CHOKE HOLD

AN ELI WOLFF THRILLER

GERALD EVERETT JONES

La Puerta Productions – Santa Monica, California

Email: bookstore@lapuerta.tv

This book is a work of fiction. Names, characters, places, and incidents either are products of the author's imagination or are used fictitiously. Any resemblance to actual events or locales or persons, living or dead, is entirely coincidental.

LaPuerta trade paperback ISBN: 978-0-9965438-3-5

EPUB ISBN: 978-1-5378439-4-0

Kindle ASIN: B07HGC2GNV

Library of Congress Control Number: 2017916582

LaPuerta Books and Media is an imprint of La Puerta Productions

www.lapuerta.tv

Author photo by Gabriella Muttone Photography, Hollywood

Cover and interior design by La Puerta Productions

For Leon

PROLOGUE

It is significant that the year was 1981 – before smartphones and pocket video, even before personal computers and the Internet. The location – the city and state – could matter to parties who might not wish this story to be told. Let's just say we're talking about a large metropolitan area somewhere in North America.

This is a work of fiction. You may think you find truth here and there. But guilty parties will take comfort in believing that what you want most is not justice but entertainment.

1

Putting a law firm above a funeral home might seem an unwise marketing decision. But the price was right on the rent. Luther "Bones" Jackson Jr. gave Lazer "Eli" Wolff a break. Originally, it was because they both liked progressive jazz. Or maybe it was because they both followed basketball, made friendly bets on games, and Bones often lost. But Eli reasoned that he only needed the place for meeting new clients, which so far wasn't all that often. He was a litigator. He belonged in court. Win a few cases and he could afford more impressive digs.

That was the plan, anyway. Until all the rest of it happened.

As for Bones, maintaining a mortuary as a storefront also had its pluses and minuses. On the plus side, having a picture window on the street was a great way to show off caskets, like so many shiny new cars. On the negative side, the clientele might think of the establishment as a kind of revolving door. If you thought about it, life was like that. But no one wanted to be reminded. Also, because Bones offered informal counseling services above and beyond those of an undertaker, locating his business on a busy street emphasized his role as an unofficial public servant.

Indeed, Bones was the godfather of the local community of color.

But the only control he had over the criminal element was what you would call moral persuasion. Eli could offer his own advice on occasion, and as with too many of his other clients, those services ended up being rendered *pro bono.*

Bones did it to keep up what you might call commercial goodwill. He was a standup guy not only for stiffs but also for their living, breathing survivors. Which, in numerous cases, included a warm widow who suddenly had control of the family checkbook. Not that he would hit on that right away. He knew how to court a lady. And Bones was a patient man.

As for Eli, his practice of law needed practice. He had no delusions about that. Collecting from a personal-injury case also required patience. It took one or two years, typically, and he did have a couple of big scores on the horizon. But meanwhile, an upstanding member of the bar had to stay out of the bars, as they say. So, Eli took on some pathetic cases. Which often came to him from Bones.

But today, Eli was expecting a paying customer in the hot seat. Divorce. Not his strong suit, but, if not too complicated, it would be mostly a paperwork hand he could play.

From the weight of her day jewelry, the silk of her too-tight top, and the prominent bulges of what surely must be silicone implants, Eli judged this babe must have some powerful reason to come to this side of the tracks to find counsel.

Eli was poised to take notes on a yellow pad, but so far all he'd jotted down was a phone number with an area code from the tonier part of town and the first name Chrissy. He guessed she had met Mr. Cadillac at a gentleman's club or perhaps a sporting event. Maybe she'd been a basketball cheerleader and he had one of those expensive courtside seats. She'd been looking for a sugar daddy, he for a trophy wife, and they'd both had sticky hands. Hers were groping in his pants for his credit cards, his inside her blouse for those artificial but perfectly shaped boobs.

Which in her aristo neighborhood was not always a recipe for true love but could be a mutually beneficial marital arrangement.

Chrissy was sobbing.

Uh oh. Here's the first danger signal, Eli thought.

Whenever they turned on the waterworks, he could feel the size of his retainer shrinking. There was bound to be a temporary problem with her cash flow. That was probably the reason she'd come over to his side of the tracks – to find a cheap lawyer. If the guy's wealth was into the millions, there were all kinds of high-toned attorneys on the right side of the tracks who would take her case on contingency. Even if her legal position was iffy, they'd at least take her on retainer, and what Amex account couldn't withstand a ten-grand hit? Answer – a card that has already been maxed out, or one that hubby was quick enough to cancel already.

So, here she was – no cash, no credit – and probably (and this was the real challenge) with no idea whatever where chubby hubby had his assets hid.

Here comes the sob story.

And Eli could decide either to walk away from the case or accept what she could scrape together now and hope he could find the loot on discovery and get enough of the settlement to not only make it all worthwhile but also top off his fee. Just now, considering his own problems with cash flow, he was inclined toward the more expedient course.

A more prudent man might have been concerned that his law practice did not focus on family law. Eli was a competent personal injury man. He knew enough about fractures, soft tissue damage, rehabilitation time, painkiller addictions, chiropractic and acupuncture alternatives, and all the gut-wrenching, subjective issues surrounding pain and suffering.

And what is divorce but an acute personal injury?

If Mrs. Cadillac could do a reasonable job helping him fill in the paperwork, he should be able to float her boat through the sewer of the county court system. It was a job-creation thing. And wasn't this part of town a bona-fide enterprise zone? Besides, Eli's pain-and-suffering antenna was picking up the strong signal that, although Chrissy might be fed up with tit squeezing, what she craved and eventually would pay dearly for was good, old-fashioned handholding.

But, as it turned out, Eli was wrong. She wasn't here about divorce at all. Since she'd walked in without an appointment, she'd been complaining about her husband's performance. Eli had made an understandable assumption about what kind of performance she was talking about. He further guessed that her litany of disappointments would culminate in her wanting to end the marriage and cash out her share of the community property.

"Mr. Wolff," she whimpered, "Since that awful accident, my

husband hasn't been able to do *anything* for a long, long time." She licked her lips and started to unbutton her blouse.

She's really overdoing it.

He'd have to get the facts straight before he could decide what to make of her come-on.

"Wait a minute," he said, gesturing to red-light her striptease. "What's this about an accident? I thought we were talking about a divorce here."

"He was injured on the job," she said. "But his employer went bankrupt."

It's personal injury after all? Hey, insurance claim or maybe workman's comp. Someone should have deep pockets. Maybe we're back in business.

And he asked, "Do you have any health insurance? If they're not paying up, we can fix that."

She sighed. "We got behind on the premiums." Then she added, undoing another button, "Please, I'll do anything."

Eli was getting a time-honored ploy for reducing the amount of his retainer. But something about this woman didn't add up.

She's dressed upscale, but somehow she and hubby failed to keep their insurance current?

Eli had trouble picturing Mr. Cadillac as the groveling employee of a company that was managed so badly it ended up in the toilet.

Unless it had been his company.

And he'd been planning to deep-six it all along.

"Let me get this straight," Eli said. "The company your husband worked for is totally defunct? Is that right?"

"Yes, I'm afraid so."

"And there's no way you could make good on that insurance? No grace period? I mean, they usually give you, like, ten days after the due date."

"No," she said. "It's lapsed. We got the letter."

"And it's not a divorce action you wish to bring?"

"Who said anything about divorce?"

Eli was still trying to figure her angle. There was a long-established Department of Labor procedure for filing workman's comp claims if the responsible company no longer existed. It was a paperwork chore, involving no court appearances, not the kind of thing he'd prefer to take on. What she needed was a paralegal at a clinic or perhaps some social worker. He had no direct experience with this type of claim, and he'd have to do some research to either get the job done or get Chrissy a referral.

But just to be sure, he asked, "Am I to understand there's no one to sue? And it's not your husband's resources you're going after to maintain your own lifestyle? You *do* plan to stay with him?"

"That's right" was all she said. Then she added as she unbuttoned still lower, wetting her lips mid-sentence, "Can't you think of any way you could, ah, waive your usual fee?"

Now, it wasn't that Eli wasn't horny. His last sexual encounter had been about as intimate as a clammy handshake, months ago with a supermarket clerk who craved a hormone flood even more than he did. It was remarkable that they'd taken precautions in the heat of the moment, but they had. He didn't even have that kind of regret to pepper the memory.

He gave her his best, insincere smile.

To which, unaccountably, she started to laugh.

"What's so funny?" he asked.

"Why," she said, "you lose! You've just been punked by Luther Jackson Junior. He was sure, if there was no money, you wouldn't take a case for love or lust, no matter how much I poured it on. Now, if you'll excuse me, I'm running late. I've got an audition for a recurring role on a soap. Bye now."

And she grabbed her purse, stood up, and hurried out.

He yelled after her, "How is that a bet? I would have stipulated as much!" But she was already out the door.

Eli didn't see the humor. And worse, as an attorney, he was particularly offended there had been no binding wager to begin with. But when in his righteous fury he tried to call Bones, all he got was the mortuary's answering service.

"Bones," he said to the recording in a low growl, "you are one sick, sorry, son of a bitch."

~

ELI WAS IMPRESSED by his friend's inventiveness and the effort it must have taken to set it up, but he was puzzled about its timing. It wasn't like they were in some grudge match and Bones was losing. They habitually bet on sporting events, especially basketball and baseball, and by Eli's reckoning Bones was temporarily ahead. Granted, Eli had just come off a long winning streak. That was during basketball season when the home team had won the championship. Since both Bones and Eli were rabid fans of the local club, all they could do honorably was bet the point spread, and Eli was the statistics man.

But tonight Bones had box-seat tickets to the baseball game, and the odds were all the other way. Born and raised in corn country, Eli was still a devoted fan of his team there, which had stayed put over the years. In his opinion, too many of the pro teams and the players in all the sports had traded venues much too often. How can a local boy find any loyalty in his heart for a team whose owner, coaches, and players have no roots in the city? If Bones weren't paying, Eli would just as soon catch a game – any game – on TV, keeping one eye on the screen and another on a mystery novel. When they bet on baseball, Bones stuck with their home team, and Eli took whatever club was visiting. Bones' favorites were winning this season, so he should have no reason to fret.

So? Why the elaborate ruse with Chrissy?

"Sheer entertainment value, my man" was all Bones said when Eli met up with him at the park.

Eli was carrying hotdogs and beer, the least he could do when his friend had somehow scored seats between the dugout and first base. He guessed Bones had some kind of connection, political or otherwise, because a box seat was not something you could just buy. It would be rented for the season, typically year after year to a business or some rich family. But on this subject, Eli was not inclined to ask questions. Not from someone who literally knows where bodies are buried.

They agreed on their small-cap bet on the game, which just as often would involve a favor rather than money. Then after a while, Eli had to ask, "Just what was so damn funny?"

Bones flashed a smile as he admitted, "I had to prove, with you, it is always, always about the money."

"You're saying I'm, what? Crass? Greedy? Ambulance chaser?"

"Not at all." He gulped his beer and laughed. "Just that you're not near horny enough, which is a matter of concern for a healthy man of your age."

Eli still didn't see the humor. "Nice seats," he huffed. "Like this makes us all homeys and shit?"

Still laughing, Bones nodded. "I coulda had hotter dates."

"Was she a hooker?"

That did it. Bones laughed so hard the corporate boys' club in the next box over shot them curious looks.

"Naw. Actors are cheaper."

"You watch," Eli said as the new hotshot pitcher squinted to get the catcher's signals. "Intentional walk."

The 3-2 pitch was high and outside, and the batter trotted off to first base.

"You're a fucking cynic, Wolff," Bones said. "And that's a fact."

That night, the home team beat the visitors 7-2, giving Eli all the more reason to think he'd fallen into a personal slump.

~

ELI WAS RENTING a one-bedroom bungalow on a block of aging tract homes located south of downtown and the university campus, just a few miles from the rapidly gentrifying black ghetto and his office above the funeral home. It was a mixed neighborhood, mostly Hispanic and solidly working-class. It wasn't necessarily safe, but then it wasn't gang turf, either. The rent was reasonable, the house was clean, the trash pickups were regular, and if there were rats, he hadn't seen any.

On this sunny morning before the holiday weekend, he was putting a loving, hand-rubbed coat of paste wax on the '69 Mustang in his driveway. Some boys were playing ball in the street. Eli looked up occasionally from his buffing to keep an eye on them. It was early and traffic was light, but kids think they will live forever.

Eli was admiring the flawless shine when Bones drove up in his classic and just as immaculately maintained Coupe de Ville.

As he hopped out of the Caddy, Bones gestured expansively toward the gleaming sports car. "What happened to that bucketa bolts you used to drive?"

"Took her down to Tijuana," Eli said proudly. "New interior, three coats of lacquer. Less than a grand, all in."

The paint was a deep, metallic orange – not exactly a Ford factory color. There were doubtlessly a few low-riders in this town with the same new paint job.

"You come into money?" Bones teased.

"New credit card," Eli shrugged.

"Careful, now. You got gambling debts, remember."

"I'm expecting a big settlement," Eli informed him. "Slip and fall in a classy department store."

Just then, they heard *CRACK!* and a hardball sailing high and hard smashed through the rear window of the Mustang.

"Damn!" Eli said, thinking immediately his new card would take another hit.

Bones reached in to pluck the ball from the back seat, and he and Eli headed off to confront the boys.

But Miguel and Ramon and their friends didn't see them coming. Those two boys were locked in a fistfight. Miguel, who looked to be about twelve, was the bigger physically, but there was plenty of fight in Ramon, who was wiry and quick, maybe younger. But he had the advantage of wielding the baseball bat.

Bones came between them, grabbed the bat, and tossed it aside as he pushed the boys apart.

"Whoaaaa," he said.

"Butt out!" yelled Miguel, eager to pound Ramon now that the bat was out of the picture.

Eli held up his hands, addressing Ramon, the only boy he knew by sight. "*Conoces la palabra* lawsuit?"

"Look out," Miguel jeered. "He's a law-yer." Apparently, this made Eli the new enemy and Miguel the new defender of innocent Ramon.

"Do you boys have the money to pay for what you did to my car?" Eli asked, and it wasn't a rhetorical question since he wasn't sure there was enough left on his card to manage it. "You plan to be rich one day?"

"Millions!" Miguel shouted, even though Eli was still focusing on Ramon on the assumption that, as the batter, he'd hit the errant ball.

Pulling a dollar bill out of his jeans, Eli turned and handed it to Miguel. "Okay, here's your million bucks."

"Yeah!" Miguel said, snatching the bill.

"What's your name?" Eli asked the smaller boy.

"Ramon."

Eli shook his hand. "Well, Ramon, I'm your attorney, Eli Wolff. And this is my associate, Mr. Jackson."

Deftly, Eli turned to Miguel, snatched the money back, and gave it to Ramon.

"Lawsuit's over. You win!" he told the smaller kid.

"Jeez!" came the cry from Miguel as it was Ramon's turn to say, "Yes!"

But now Eli plucked the bill from Ramon, quickly tore it in half, handed one piece back to Ramon, and kept the other half for himself.

"You gotta pay my fee."

Ramon was staring disheartened at the torn bill when Eli grabbed it again, tore off a postage-stamp-sized piece, and gifted the scrap ceremonially to Ramon.

"I had expenses," he explained.

The boys were still trying to make sense of the civics lesson as Eli pointed to the Mustang. "You guys are going to work this off. Ramon, I'll be having a talk with your mother."

Bones gave the ball back to Ramon, whose guilty look made further fact-finding unnecessary.

As he and Eli walked back to the house, Bones grinned. "Nice work back there, counselor."

"I guess I'm not exactly telling them the legal system works."

"You know what they say."

"No, what do they say?"

"Those who can't do – teach."

2

Bones' crack about teaching stung because Eli had been considering doing just that. He wasn't thinking about changing professions. He'd just take on some volunteer work to keep himself out of the bars, as the expression goes.

Eli had met Vince Dipego at the Police Youth League, a community outreach program sanctioned by the department. At the PYL gym, cops and kids played basketball. Social workers and public defenders occasionally got tapped as subs for the overworked cops, and that's how Eli happened to be on the court one night. Dipego, a parole officer, had reached out to him about doing some pro bono legal work. He declined at the time because he was working for free too much already. Most of Eli's paying clients weren't paying.

You could say Eli was bored. That was partly it. As for whatever free time he could manage, dating seemed like asking for grief. He wasn't retired from the game, but just now he wasn't about to go scouting. As many workaholics do, he nursed the faint hope that he'd collide with a new prospect in the performance of his daily professional routine. A few times, he'd thought about calling Keiko on impulse. But asking for more rejection was no plan at all. And dialing drunk, in the wee hours when he was most inclined to try, might help him say what he felt but would not win him her sympathy.

No, Eli's motivations had more to do with his accidental meetup with Ramon. Here was a kid, lived in his neighborhood, he'd never met. What kind of prospects did this boy have? Was he learning anything at school? What did he want to be when he grew up, and how wildly unlikely was that goal for him in this town, in this society? Had he ever been approached by a gang member? Did he know anyone who was in a gang? Or serving time?

When would it be too late for him?

"So what kind of trouble do you want to get into?" Vince asked Eli on the phone when he called.

"What've you got?" Eli asked (bravely, he thought).

"I'm assuming you still don't want to do legal counseling, and you frankly suck at basketball."

"Guilty and guilty."

"What's driving this?"

"I want to know these kids better," Eli said. "I had a run-in with a young one the other day. I'd like to help him, but I don't know how. Seems like I need to see where he could be headed before I go charging in there. You know how, if you don't know what you're doing, acting with good intentions can make things worse? My high-school English teacher freshman year was the chairman of the department. He'd spent years teaching seniors, and he saw how screwed up they were. So he decided he'd take over the freshman classes — correct their mistakes before those became bad habits. But he could only do that because he'd already spent time with the seniors, seen exactly where they were challenged."

From Vince came an audible sigh. "Well, if you think you're going to change the world, think again."

"Isn't that what you're trying to do?"

"Never mind me. I get lots of double overtime and great benefits. What do you expect to get?"

"I get to wear myself out even more than usual. Then maybe I can skip the sleeping pills." Eli wasn't on drugs, at least not yet, but he did spend too much time watching movie reruns on late-night TV.

"No girlfriends in the picture?" Vince was smiling, Eli was sure.

"How do you know, and why do you care?"

"Because women tend to not only keep a man busy, but they spend enough of his money that he's desperate to earn more. A guy in a committed relationship doesn't go looking for volunteer work."

"Again, guilty," Eli said. "Come on, there must be something."

"Sure," Vince said. "I'm just trying to qualify the request, you might say. So, just to be clear, this is not about meeting women?"

"Is that what you do at A-A?"

"You don't get to jerk *my* chain, Lazer," Vince chuckled. "I just need to know where you're coming from."

"I told you," Eli said. "I don't know enough to make my request more specific."

"Funny you should bring up English composition," Vince said. "You any good at that?"

"I can spell. Hell, I can *type.*"

"But can you tell a story?" Vince wanted to know. "I mean, without gulping down two drinks first."

"I can manage. Sure."

"I'm not connected with the kids in the youth camps or the ones on probation. Different department. And besides, when it's kids, some of the higher-ups get their panties in a twist about whether you've got a teaching certificate. But, for some of my guys, we've got this halfway house. Mostly young guys, mostly convicted of nonviolent crimes. They're not kids anymore, but they messed up before they could get any work experience. And if you ever do tutor the younger ones, it won't do you any harm to understand what they could face when they get older. Out in the world, what are they going to do? Wash pots or bus tables. Unless they decide, what-the-hell, they'll go back to grand theft or selling dope. The best thing we can do for them is push them to get their GED, high-school equivalence. We need instructors for English comp and math. I presume you suck at math."

"It wasn't my best subject."

"Nor mine. But we got a guy for that. Chinese, what else?"

"So, you want me to teach English comp?" Eli asked.

"Storytelling, my man. You ask them to write something on current affairs, news headlines, you're going to get blank looks and blanker paper. But you ask for their story – they all got stories – you might get something."

"Sounds like therapy."

"Damn straight. You get them to open up, you might find out a lot more than whether they can spell."

3

It was the day before the long Labor Day weekend. (We're still in 1981.) The forecast was for hot and sticky, which to patrol officers Norbert Oates and Rob Torres meant citizens could be drunk and angry even more than usual. As the cops cruised the crowded surface streets in their black-and-white Gran Fury, they were on the lookout for drivers who were in too much of a hurry, weaving, or just driving too slow. It was mid-afternoon. Workers who had taken off early for the weekend had already cashed their checks and hit the bars.

And, sure enough, here was a guy who had trouble staying in his lane.

After they switched on their MARS lights, the guy drove on for a block and a half before he pulled off the busy boulevard and into an alley, where he stopped. The car was a battered Ford Falcon, so they weren't expecting a pimp or a dealer. Probably a guy who'd already drunk his paycheck.

Oates stood behind the open passenger door of the patrol car as Torres ordered the perp out of the Ford. The guy was short, scrawny, ebony-skinned, and wearing a do-rag.

But he was no drunk. He couldn't stop twitching.

Torres had the guy face away from him and place his hands on the roof of the car. Oates could tell he was having trouble taking simple directions. His erratic movements were worrisome. Clearly, he was strung out, but the question was, how would he react? He didn't seem hostile so much as confused.

Torres was taking it slow. Fine. But the guy couldn't keep his hands from fidgeting. Oates couldn't hear what they were saying, but he saw the man was gesturing with them as he answered Torres.

Suddenly, the guy jerked around, one arm outstretched as if in appeal, the other dropping to his hip. Oates judged the outstretched arm was too close to Torres, feared he was going for his partner's sidearm, and the senior cop drew his weapon.

Torres, who should have been standing to the side, had his back to Oates, in the line of fire.

"Get clear!" yelled Oates.

Torres and the perp were doing a dance now. The perp's other hand went from his hip into his pants pocket.

"Dammit, Torres!"

Torres spun around toward Oates, still blocking the shot. He now appeared to be protecting the perp as he gave his partner a push-back gesture.

"It's his wallet, Bert. He went for his wallet."

The perp was waving both hands in the air now, having dropped the wallet. He was whimpering.

Torres bent down to pick up the wallet. That move also baffled Oates, but he holstered his gun.

They called for the Ford to be towed. Then they took the guy in and booked him on DUI for drug intoxication, which took most of the afternoon.

By the time they left the station, there were still three hours left on the day watch. As they were about to climb back into the patrol car, Oates indicated he wanted the driver's side. Torres, who had driven through the morning hours, hoped that getting behind the wheel would calm his partner down.

They'd only been riding together for a few months, but Torres already knew Oates was a fanatic about control. Torres was a lean, Marine Corps vet who'd recently joined the department after two tours in Vietnam. He was even-tempered and capable. And he could take orders. But in Oates' estimation, Rob was a probationer, a green recruit. Oates had been on the ghetto beat for fifteen years, during which time he'd changed partners more frequently than most. He was a big man with swagger, and he didn't suffer fools. He knew the street, and he'd made his place on it. These young cops may have gotten high marks at the academy, and, like Torres, they might even be war heroes, but too often they didn't know any better than to go faithfully by the book.

Oates knew procedure, and he could cite you chapter and verse. But, if you wanted to stay alive in this job, you had to learn when to trust your gut. Take, for example, the lessons learned by their colleagues, the state troopers. When those guys were in training on the firing range, it was drilled into them to pick up their spent shell casings and pocket them before reloading the next magazine. And over the years there had been more than one case of dead troopers, found outgunned by the side of the road, their left hands in the pockets of their nancy jodhpurs, still clutching eight empty shells.

Oates favored his gut, which, if he were to be honest, was starting to bulge over his belt. The city's officers prided themselves on their military-style physical fitness. Most of them looked like Torres – crewcut, slender, and fresh-pressed. These days, as he was pushing forty, Oates feared he was beginning to look like a doughy flatfoot.

They resumed their patrol near the alley where they'd made the arrest, and they drove by to make sure the druggie's Falcon had in fact been taken to the impound yard.

Oates' style when he was angry, like now, was to shut up. It was Torres' job, he figured, to know what he did wrong. And if he didn't know, he'd better learn – fast.

Torres finally broke the silence. "What happened back there?"

"You nearly got yourself shot in the back is what happened back there."

"Why did you draw on him?"

"Are you kidding me? He was all over the place. For all I knew, he was trying to grab your weapon."

"Not even close," Torres said.

"Then he goes for his goddamn pocket? For all I knew, he had a knife! You think of that?"

Torres went quiet and took a breath before he spoke again. He didn't want Oates getting more upset. "Looking back on it, there was more chance of you shooting me. That guy would have trouble putting his socks on."

"Okay, Rob," Oates said. "You think I'm the wild one, like I make it up as I go along? You want to talk procedure? Your position was all wrong."

"It's not like that perp was standing still!"

"Even when he was getting out of the car, you had your back to me."

"I had to step back, or he could have hit me with the car door."

"Is that what really happened, or is that how you're telling it?"

"I'm being honest," Torres said. "With due respect, sir."

"Okay, there was a lot going on, not your usual stop. But let's say the situation was reversed. You covering me. Shit like that comes down, can I count on you to act fast enough I'm not gonna be dead?"

IN THE MORNING briefing at the station, the watch commander had emphasized how dangerous was the combination of the heat, the holiday weekend, binge drinking, and domestic firearms. As a usual precaution, public service ads on TV and radio – as well as billboards all over the city in two languages – warned against firing weapons into the air in celebration. People somehow forgot that what goes up must come down. Those bullets don't go into orbit – they can kill a child miles away, where there isn't even a drive-by perpetrator to blame for the family's lifelong grief.

"That open window makes me nervous," Oates complained. Their cruiser didn't have air conditioning.

"I gotta have some air," Torres said.

"Procedure says leave it up," Oates shot back. "You wanna take a brick in the head?"

And then because the window was open, they distinctly heard what sounded like a barrage of small-arms fire.

Oates stepped on the accelerator, flipped on the MARS lights and siren, and took the next corner hard.

"Holy shit," he said. "Call it in."

They drove in the direction of the sound, even though there might be no way to identify its source. But just a block and a half away, a crowd that had gathered at an apartment complex drew their attention. It was a block party of about fifty people, African-Americans of all ages. They were gathered in the courtyard of a two-story building around smoking barbecues. A lot of them were congregating on the second-floor balcony, where several apartments doors were propped open.

Among the facts later established, a large, muscular black man named Hank Ellis, age twenty-nine, was standing in the middle of that courtyard lecturing a group of kids. He was easy to spot in his red T-shirt. From the balcony, his scrawny cousin Danny Ellis was looking down on the party as he nuzzled his flashy girlfriend Cyndi. He was in a good position to see what the kids had been doing to deserve a scolding from Hank.

What happened next was a fast-paced blur.

The patrol car careened into the courtyard and screeched to a stop. Its doors flew open, and out came officers Rob Torres with his riot gun at the ready and Bert Oates, who had drawn his sidearm with one hand and was clutching the P. A. mic with the other.

"All right!" Oates yelled over the P. A. "Who fired that weapon?"

The crowd didn't panic. Far from being intimidated, most of them seemed annoyed, and some were angry. The angry voices came all at once:

"For-get it!"

"No gun!"

"Fire crackers, understand?"

"This is a *party*, man."

"Hey, go *home!*"

"Son of a bitch!"

"What *is* this?"

From the balcony, Danny Ellis was heard to yell at the cops, "Hey, chill! Nobody got a gun here!"

From the ground near the patrol car where he stood with the kids, Hank turned slowly to look up at Danny. Then, his back to the cops, the big man calmly climbed the stairs.

Oates shouted after him, "You! Hold it right there!"

But Hank ignored him and kept on climbing, two steps at a time.

The light of day was fading rapidly, and poor visibility is one reason why there was a difference of opinion about what happened next.

The officers say they saw a glint of metal in Hank's right hand. No one in the crowd that day could confirm this, and people close to Hank swore he didn't own a gun – as far as they knew.

But, apparently thinking Hank was armed, Oates brought his weapon up to track the man's ascent up the stairs. But in the twilight there was no clear sight of a gun, and, as people shoved past each other on the stairs, Oates had no clear shot even if he had seen a gun.

Oates then ran to the foot of the stairs, where he hesitated long enough for Torres to pump the shotgun and move behind to cover him.

When he was on the balcony, Hank turned and shouted something at Oates. The officer shouted something back. There are multiple and conflicting versions about what was said.

According to witnesses, Hank then disappeared inside his own apartment, where he closed the door. Oates never climbed the stairs.

The officers lowered their weapons. One of the kids came over to Torres and showed him a handful of firecracker ash and charred paper casings.

The officers climbed back into the patrol car, switched off the MARS lights, and drove off. If they had called for backup, none arrived. It was a busy night, for all concerned. The party resumed, but the kids were sent home, and no more fireworks were detonated.

FOUR HOURS LATER –

On his living room floor, facedown and just outside the bathroom, lay the lifeless body of Hank Ellis. A puddle of blood about the size of a pie plate had soaked into the carpet around his head.

The room was full of men – none of them black. There were two detectives, a photographer, a forensics technician, and a coroner's deputy who was unfolding a body bag.

Three other men were there. In charge of the scene was Lt. Delbert Hughes, a hardened former drill instructor and head of Homicide Division. He conferred briefly with Oates and Torres, then dismissed them with a warning that they were not to discuss what happened with anyone – not even Internal Affairs – without further advice from him.

Then Hughes strode into the kitchen and placed a call:

"We have a situation down here."

4

It was the middle of the night after Hank's death, and Norbert Oates could not sleep. For an old building, his apartment was spacious – there were three bedrooms. Two of them were empty.

He didn't feel much like doing a load of laundry. He'd already rinsed off his dinner plate and put the silverware in a cup of soapy water – his practical approach to keeping a clean kitchen.

He figured a hit of caffeine would not prevent him from the sleep he wasn't getting. So, he made a cup of instant coffee, sat down at the kitchen table, and wrote this letter:

Dear Lucille,

I know you'd expect me to call, but there's never a good time. Besides, I'll do better writing on this note paper. If I make a fool of myself, I can always wad it up, and you'll never see it. On the phone you can never take back the words no matter how much you apologize. Then there are the long-distance charges. It's not like you don't have bills, too, but I'm glad I can still make the rent in a decent part of town.

We haven't spoken since you phoned to say that Bradley arrived safe and sound. I know my decision was kind of abrupt, but I'm sure under the circumstances this is the best thing for him. Clara's passing was hard on all of us, and we tried to shield him from too many details. There toward the last, when I took him to visit her in the hospice, she had a couple of bright days, and we didn't let him stay long. He never saw her in pain. He seemed numb through it all, and that concerns me. I bet he gets this "big boys don't cry" thing from me. Frankly, I wish he'd bawled his eyes out. There were times I did, but he never saw.

He was eight on his last birthday. You probably knew that — what with you being so faithful about sending him a card every year. But if you ask him, he'll say he's ten. Bottom line, a boy at that age needs a mother more than a father. Jack is a good man, more mild-mannered than me. I don't expect him to train Brad to use a shotgun, but maybe they could go fishing now and then. Mostly he'll need someone to talk to, especially as he gets into his teens. Your husband didn't ask for this (neither did you), but I know you both love the boy, and that's what counts.

Another big reason for the decision was his schooling. The big-city schools here are warehouses for gangbangers. It's amazing they can teach anything. Then there are two types of private school — snob academies with tuition beyond my reach and little warehouses that aren't as expensive but full of slackers, along with seriously disturbed kids who are between gigs in private mental health programs. I confess I didn't research your local situation, but I am certain your rural schools have to be a better experience for him. Even if it's just getting more personal attention.

Here they said he could be ADHD, but they didn't go through with the testing. In this monster system, just getting an appointment with a psych worker could take weeks – or longer. (If he was in a wheelchair, I bet they'd see him right away!) But what are they going to do? Put him on Ritalin? He'd be even more of a zombie than he pretends to be now. Not talking, not willing to express himself?

Diet and exercise, like my doctor says but I don't do. Maybe that's what he needs. Something healthier than a corndog in the microwave.

So do let me know about his school and how he's doing. Maybe just a message on the answering machine. I won't be looking over your shoulder or his. Not that I wouldn't want the details, but I don't want you to feel like I'd second-guess. I trust you, and you probably know better than me what's right.

Clara had some money in the bank for him. I'll send it to you, lump sum. No need to dole it out. He probably needs clothes.

Another reason for the decision. I don't have to tell you my work is dangerous. There are a lot of close calls. But something happened today. Almost thought it would be my last. Right after we lost Clara, I saw the lawyer and got my will updated. So I'll mail that with the check. If on the other hand I get wounded, I'll be in the hospital or flying a desk. Either way, we get pretty good benefits, so expenses should be mostly covered.

I expect you're going to tell me again I should think about quitting. I'm six years away from fully vested retirement. I plan to stay in at least that long. Odd thing. Guys on the force who retire don't live that long afterwards. They don't even make it through their sixties. Maybe the stress keeps us alive?

Thank you. I can never repay.

Your loving brother,

Bert

5

Jessie's was a jazz club in the heart of the community. It was named after its owner, actress and comedienne Jessica B. The place would become known for its world-class improvisational musicians – ranging from straight-ahead to progressive to no-label to ad hoc – and its classic, home-cooked menu featuring fried chicken, corn on the cobb, collard greens cooked in lard, mashed potatoes, redeye gravy, and corn bread slathered with butter and honey.

And she stocked a full bar, with an extensive list of mixed drinks. But then what would a gentleman want but bourbon?

Eli had first heard Bones play at a different club, The Orleans, a swanky Cajun-style joint over in a white-neighborhood-adjacent district. Eli was so impressed with the tenor sax player's riffs that he threw ten bucks in the tip jar. That got a conversation started when the band was packing up, and then they matched shots of Old Fitzgerald at the bar until closing time.

Jessie's, which had just opened, was their new favorite hangout. The groups were fresher, played less coverage and more originals. But in either place, most of the band members who weren't headliners were moonlighting from legit orchestras and sound stages. Bones had been playing the sax since he was ten. He started on the alto, a horn more appropriate to his size, but in his teens, as he grew to the height of nearly a basketball center, he took up the big, honking tenor. The horn had a raw, braying voice that suited him.

And, the other thing about Jessie's, perhaps because of her stardom – there were a few more white faces in the crowd. Not that Eli cared. But sometimes Bones worried his friend looked like a wannabe person of color, an inside-out Oreo cookie, a honky who was too eager to study tap.

In fact, Eli was a closet Jew. His father was a Wolfowicz who had changed it to Wolff because, in retailing years ago, some buyers would not give appointments to manufacturers' reps with Semitic last names. Wolff might be Jewish, but it might not. It had been a common name in Germany for centuries. But Eli knew that the Wolfowiczs had been Polish and that the Nazis had imprisoned some of them. As to his given name Lazer, it was the diminutive Yiddish name for Eliezer. His parents always called him Eli, and he didn't know anything about the other names until he was five and an uncle asked him why they weren't having him learn Hebrew so he'd be prepared for his bar mitzvah. He did end up with a sparse education in the language, enough to get through the ceremony, which he remembered mainly because it was the only time in his life when smiling people handed him cash without his asking for it. So, devout he wasn't.

Eli couldn't pass as black, but people might have taken him for a WASP. Now, he didn't represent himself that way – he was no Wonder Bread Episcopalian – but he didn't advertise his heritage, either. He was fair-haired and even had a few freckles. And he had what some people would think of as an All-American jawline and nose. Besides, "Jewish lawyer" was not exactly a winning stereotype, even in those presumably enlightened times. To himself, he was proud of his background. He'd studied the Torah as a boy, all the way through to his *bar mitzvah*. He could read a bit of Hebrew and say a few words, and he knew when to sit and when to stand and *shuckle* in temple. He even carried his secret ethnicity into his love of baseball. His all-time favorite player was Al Rosen, "the Hebrew Hammer," the legendary third baseman during the 1950s for the Cleveland Indians.

Eli and Bones were an unlikely pair. They were best buds at the worst of times in one of the most chaotic melting pots on the planet. The black community here was larger than the population of all races in some other big cities. But even if blacks and whites held each other at arm's length over the sheer expanse of the sprawling city, there was now a third race to contend with – the Latinos were showing up in droves. Many of them couldn't even speak English, but they were underbidding everyone for menial jobs. In the old days, working as a busboy in a restaurant wasn't a job for an African-American unless he'd done prison time and couldn't find anything else. But nowadays, patrons understood that the difference between a busboy and a waiter was that the busboy spoke only Spanish and smiled a lot.

The staff at Jessie's was as all-black as a private club on the other side of town might be all-white. Nobody was complaining.

Tonight, it was officially the holiday weekend, and the house was packed with reservations. Bones and his crew were improvising on "Smoke Gets in Your Eyes." And if the emotion in the music didn't bring tears, the dense, low-hanging smoke in the room would. The set wasn't so much coverage as a starting-off place for a languid contemplation of the blues itself.

When Bones ended his solo with a fanfare in an extremely righteous manner, the diners looked up from their smothered plates and applauded with obvious enthusiasm. He'd touched nerves. His raw sax was the voice of an animal crying in the wilderness, a hibernating bear waking with a groan, a bull craving a heifer – a man wondering why he'd practiced a difficult skill for two decades so he could play smoke-filled rooms for nickels and dimes.

But when he stepped off the stage to join Eli at his table, he looked genuinely depressed. Eli figured it wasn't the music. Blues didn't get him down, and righteous playing usually brought a shameless grin.

"What's wrong?" Eli asked as Bones plunked himself down. "You killed up there."

Eli had made sure to order Bones his drink neat, with soda back. Good jazz and all that blowing inspire a thirst.

Bones knocked the double shot back in a gulp and sighed, "People come to me. Like a mortician is supposed to know more than them about life and death? There's some nasty shit going down."

Eli tried to shrug it off. "Uh-oh. Is this where I say, 'Can I help?'"

"The cops killed a brother yesterday. Unarmed, in his own home."

"This is another joke, right?"

Bones shot him a look that said cut the crap.

"Not renta-cops or security guards? As in the cops on *the force*? You want us to fight City Hall?"

Bones could bet against me on this one, with slam-dunk odds.

"Meet his widow. Marcia. First girl I ever kissed. I was nine. She was thirteen." Then Bones added, "But not in your jive-ass office. You'll use mine. And wear a tie that doesn't look like somebody spilled paint on it."

To WEAR with his gray suit, he'd found a blue tie with a conservative, muted pattern. It was too wide or too narrow, he didn't know which. But at least it had no gravy stains. The suit trousers were too tight. He'd put on a couple of inches at the waist since college. But he managed to get them zipped up. Most of the time he'd be sitting behind the desk, and he hoped when he stood in greeting it wouldn't be for long.

On Monday morning, there was Eli, sitting behind an elegant walnut desk that bore the plaque, "Luther Jackson Jr. – Funeral Director."

Marcia Ellis sat opposite him in a prim, print dress. Behind her on a couch were her two small children, Lon and Janet, who were remarkably quiet, as if sitting in church.

She acted as if she were the one on trial. "I wasn't there," she said flatly. "Danny was. Hank's cousin."

Eli tried a reassuring smile. "I'm not the cops, okay?" Then he indicated the kids and asked her quietly, "Should they be in here?"

"They know," Marcia sniffed. "At least they weren't there to see it. I was at my mother's with them."

"You and Hank had a fight?"

This could be a show-stopper. Husbands and wives had their good days and bad. But if Ellis was known to have a quick temper — or if, God forbid, he was a wife-batterer — they might as well forget it.

"No," she said. "But he got so he wouldn't talk. He was so keyed up with that employee of the year thing. I thought he better be by himself for a while."

"He and Danny were, what, watching a game?"

She sniffed again. "Having a party, would be my guess. Danny had his tramp girlfriend over. Cyndi. Lord knows who else."

"Do you think Hank was intoxicated? Did he drink a lot?"

"If he drank, he'd fall asleep. My husband was never mean."

Good. We might stand a chance. And he was employee of the year? Almost?

Eli had to explain, "If they killed an unarmed, innocent man, the city should compensate you for your loss. Not that money can do much, but it's all anyone can do at this point. We need to have a coroner's inquest. That is, we have to try to get them to hold an inquest. Which I understand they don't always do. Especially when they have reasons for not doing it."

He could tell from her glazed look he'd lost her. She didn't want to know the details. But he had to make sure she understood. "If the coroner decides it was an accident, they won't pay."

"Whatever" was all she said.

"Mrs. Ellis, what I'm saying is, there could be money, but don't count on it."

"Is that what you think I want? You need some, I guess." She glanced at the plaque. "Get yourself your own office."

"I get a third of whatever I get for you. If we both decide to go ahead. You don't pay me anything now, and I only get money if you do."

She hesitated. "I told Mr. Jackson I want a lawyer that's one of us. And he brings me to you! So I don't know."

"Why did Bones recommend me, do you think?"

"He says you're like a terrier. You take hold of a thing, and you don't let go." She must have believed as much and was reassured, to a point. But her eyes were getting moist. "Can you make my home safe for us to live in? How are we gonna sleep at night?"

"Believe me, the police have no reason to go back there. They'd just as soon you went on with life." Her head was down, and he bent to look her in the face. "But we can't, can we? I'm not as big as some dogs, but I have a really annoying bark. And sooner or later, they pay attention. Then they pay."

She managed a smile. "What I want is justice for Hank. I want his children to know he was a good man."

"Okay," Eli said. "I should hear what Danny has to say. Where can I find him?"

"County jail," she said.

And he's our credible witness?

"He's not in for this," she clarified. "Danny can get into trouble on his own."

6

The city's central jail was a huge red-brick facility downtown. It was supposed to provide short-term incarceration for suspects who were awaiting trial or who, having been convicted, either had drawn short sentences or were waiting to be transferred into the state prison system. But the place was perpetually overcrowded, transfers could take forever, and conditions were so bad that some reporters alleged "The Tank" was one of the ten worst prisons in the world. True or not, some men went in and never came out.

Marcia had no specifics on why they were holding Danny. Eli figured, rather than spend time on hold on the phone to the sheriff's department, he'd better just go down there and pay a visit. Material witness or protective custody – either or both of those could apply to Danny. But neither justified throwing him in the Stink Tank.

Unless there was nobody to object and this inconvenient person could conveniently disappear.

Eli took a seat on the other side of the thick Plexiglas in a visitation room. A guard brought Danny in. He looked fresh-scrubbed, but his right arm was in a sling. He was a scrawny dude, with a nervousness that might have less to do with his present circumstances than with drug withdrawal.

Before Eli could introduce himself, Danny announced loudly, "I got nothing to tell."

Okay, so he's scared. Who wouldn't be?

Eli tried the reassuring smile but just as quickly let it drop. It would take more than a pleasant bedside manner to make this guy talk.

"Why are they holding you?"

Danny shrugged as if to say, *Do they need a reason?*

"This is bullshit," Eli fumed. He got up and signaled to the guard the interview was over.

THE DISCHARGE FORMALITIES took more than an hour, but when Eli finally left the building, he took Danny with him.

"How'd you do that, man?" Danny seemed genuinely impressed to have made friends with a white guy who could actually work the system.

"There's a law that says they can't keep you in there without a good reason," Eli explained. "They like to forget that rule, but if you remind them in the right way, like inform them you'll get a judge to decide, suddenly they remember their manners."

"Oh, they got a reason," Danny confided. "I saw what those motherfuckers did to Hank."

"Okay, here's the deal," Eli told him. "You tell it all to me, and I buy you a sandwich."

That brought a smile. They found a hotdog vendor on the next block, and Danny ordered three with the works and a barrel-sized soda to wash it down. They sat on the edge of a planter on the sidewalk, and Eli had to coax Danny into chewing before he swallowed, making sure there was nothing lodged in his throat as he talked.

For a guy who had nothing to tell, he had a helluva story.

TWO HOURS BEFORE THE INCIDENT, Hank was completing his shift at the Breezway Motel, where he worked in the laundry room. Danny had promised to meet up with him so he could be his cousin's guest for the annual employee awards party. In the last few months, a supervisor who'd given Hank high performance ratings had let him believe he could expect some major recognition.

All Danny had told the desk clerk on his arrival was that he was there to pick up Hank. Neither of them knew whether it was allowed for Hank to have a guest at the function. But Hank figured, if they'd be giving him an award, how could they say no?

No one bothered to escort Danny as he took the service elevator to the basement. There he found Hank in the noisy, steamy laundry room, where he hefted a huge bundle of fresh towels.

"Four o'clock!" Danny announced. "I said I be here! And on the fucking dot!"

Hank was pleased to see him but wouldn't show it. "How'd you get in?" was all he said.

"I said I come to see the employee of the year!" Which wasn't true, but Danny wanted to pump his fighter up before the big match. Stone-faced Hank had better be able to manage a grateful smile when they gave him whatever they were going to give him.

"I got stuff to do first," Hank said as he hoisted a bundle to his other broad shoulder and strode off to load up a row of housekeeping carts.

"That's right, Hank," Danny said gleefully. "They got to wait for *you* now!"

After the chore was done, Hank led him to a back stairway, which led up to the wait staff passageway to the kitchen and the main dining room.

As he panted to keep up with the big man's stride, Danny asked him, "What do you suppose you get? Gold watch?"

There was a pause as if Hank hadn't heard. Then he said simply, "They don't do that."

They made their way through the kitchen, which was empty. Everyone must already be at the ceremony.

Hank had his hand on the pushbar of the service door when he flashed a grin and said, "Bonus. They give you a bonus."

"All those double shifts? It's got to be large!"

They could hear applause and laughter on the other side.

Hank swung the door open wide, ready to claim his rightful prize.

There on the dais in front of the assembled staff was twenty-something Kimberly Livingston. She was being kissed on an upturned cheek by balding, fifty-something Ed Sikes, the hotel manager.

Ignoring political correctness, the employees were singing, "For She's a Jolly Good Fellow."

"This is fucked, man," Danny muttered.

Sikes caught sight of Hank. His face went slack for an instant, then he beckoned him over with what he must have thought was a generous wave.

But Hank didn't move.

"This is fucked, man."

HANK DIDN'T ACKNOWLEDGE his defeat to Danny. He just turned and walked back through the kitchen, grabbed his lunch pail from his locker, and went home. Danny, who didn't have a car and had taken the bus to the motel, rode with him.

At the apartment complex, the barbecues were already fired up. As Hank took a shower, Danny used the phone to call Cyndi and invite her over to the party. He told her Marcia was away with the kids and Hank could use some company, too. He asked her to bring beer and promised Hank would pay her back.

After Hank had a change of clothes, Danny thought he saw him relax. They went out on the balcony to survey the party.

"It's fucked, that's all," Danny said and just as quickly realized Hank was already past it. "Look, Cyndi's here!" he said, as he saw her make her way through the crowd to the stairs. She had her hottie friend Theresa with her, who from her droopy eyes and faltering step looked to be stoned already. "She got her friend with her – the fox! Fuck the motel, man. Fuck the fox!"

"I'm a family man, you forget," Hank said quietly. "She's your guest, you do what you want. But she gets out of line with me, she's not welcome in my house. You understand?"

Hank had been watching a group of preteen boys who were pushing and shoving each other down below. One of them lit a string of firecrackers, and they played a game of chicken passing it back and forth until one threw it on the ground just before it exploded. Hank pushed past people on the stairs as he went down to break it up. They'd already lit another string when he grabbed it and threw it to the curb.

As a half-dozen ladyfingers went off in the gutter, Hank pulled the oldest boy over to him. "Michael, you too intelligent for this dumb-ass shit. I'm ashamed of you. All of you. Let me have what you got." The boys handed over their fireworks, which Hank shoved in his pocket.

He was about to head back up the stairs when the patrol car pulled in, the armed officers jumped out, and the crowd shouted jeers.

Hank turned to Oates, who was no more than five feet away.

"You better get your white faces out of here, or you're going to get hurt," he said.

He didn't wait for a response and turned to stride up the stairs to the balcony. Hank seemed unhurried, didn't acknowledge that the officer had a weapon trained on his back.

It wasn't until he'd reached the balcony that he turned back and stared straight at the upraised gun.

Still at the bottom of the stairs, Oates called up, "You got something to say, boy?"

Torres closed his distance to Oates, and now the riot gun was also pointed at Hank. All of the raised faces looked to the big man who was standing up to the cops.

Hank spat out, "You the boy in my neighborhood, *boy.*" And he turned and walked back into his apartment. Danny, Cyndi, and Theresa followed him in, and the door closed.

~

IN THE APARTMENT – it couldn't have been more than fifteen minutes later – they'd popped open the beers Cyndi brought. Danny had turned on the TV, and Theresa had gone back out, perhaps because she hoped someone else at the party had something harder than beer to trade for her favors.

Nobody said anything for a while as Danny flipped through the channels. Then he looked up and said admiringly to Hank, "Magnificent, man! Sweet Jesus!"

As if announcing she might not stay long either, Cyndi mumbled, "Theresa, she want none of this. Some party."

Ignoring her, Hank got up and went into the bathroom, where he left the door open long enough to call back to Danny, "Lock us in. My key's in the door."

"That's smart, Hank," Danny said as he got up. He was about to pull the outer protective door grille closed and reached around to pull the key from the deadbolt.

Just then, a police baton swung down hard on his forearm.

"Ahhhhh!"

Oates tore into the apartment, pushing Danny aside and taking wide swings with the club. Torres was right behind him with club drawn, but not swinging. Cyndi screamed and ran past them out the door.

Danny yelled, "Hank! Hank, they in here! They in here!"

Then he ran out.

DANNY WAS FINISHING A FOURTH DOG, this one smothered with chili, which was all over his face. Eli had to make a third trip back to the vendor to get more napkins.

As Danny cleaned up, Eli asked him, "Did Hank even own a gun?"

"He'd be alive today if he did."

"They murdered him for talking back?"

"For disrespecting them. They hate that."

"But you didn't actually see them do it?"

"Do I look stupid enough to hang around there?"

This was all useful information, hard evidence. Danny's testimony could prove that the police returned to the apartment after having left the scene. And they'd injured him on the way in. It was pretty clear they were intent on revenge, not reacting in their own defense. An inquest would stop short of fixing blame for the killing. But the strong suggestion that the cops had gone in there intending to punish Hank couldn't be ignored.

"Did anybody else see it?" Eli asked.

Danny looked away as he said, "Don't think so."

The medics at the jail had done a decent job of putting Danny's broken arm in a cast. That might be a matter to be pursued, but not now. Danny assured Eli that he wouldn't go back to Cyndi's place, where he'd been living, but he'd stay at a friend's, where he hoped he'd be safe. Even though getting lost might be a safer plan, Eli cautioned him not to leave town.

Eli walked Danny to the bus stop, where he gave him carfare and then some. He gave him a business card and told him to call any time if he could think of anything or anyone else.

Or if anyone threatened him.

Eli had parked the Mustang a few blocks away in a structure. He could have used the underground parking facility at the jail, but he wasn't so much fearful about leaving the car there as he was concerned about the safety of his own person. He liked the idea that he could walk out the door of that awful place – into sunlight and freedom – and keep on walking.

He wondered whether he was being followed. If the city's infamous secret police division was on him, he figured he'd never see them. They'd use teams of watchers dressed like ordinary citizens who could track him from a combination of moving and stationary vantage points – following, oncoming, and intersecting, as well as observing from street level or high above. Or, at least, that's how the professional spies were said to do it in those thrillers written by ex-spies.

But there was also the thought that buddies of the cop perpetrators might want to deal with him in some nasty, unofficial capacity. That was the more worrisome possibility.

Arriving at the structure, he circled the block first. Then he took the elevator to the top floor and made his way back down to the second floor by the back stairs. On that floor, he crouched down and then darted between the rows of cars until he could peek over a hood to get a glimpse of the Mustang.

There was no one lurking around it, and the steering-wheel lock looked undisturbed. And in his needlessly serpentine approach, he hadn't encountered another human being.

But Eli was a child of the 'Sixties. In his student days, there was a saying:

Paranoia is just a heightened state of awareness.

All the same, he thought it best to avoid going home. There was a packed suitcase in his trunk. He'd already asked to bunk with Bones, at least until the inquest was over – if there was to be one.

But first he had to pay a visit to an ex-girlfriend.

7

Nervous mothers, mostly Chicana, sat holding their children in the crowded waiting room of the Mendes Charity Health Clinic. The kids were infants and toddlers. The healthier ones were fidgeting and vocalizing their distress, ranging from whimpers to screams. The still, quiet ones were likely to be seriously ill.

Unnoticed by its teenage mother who had a squirming infant in her arms, a one-year-old rooted in her open purse to find a stick pen, the kind with a removable cap.

Seconds later, the kid was choking, and his mother was yelling, "My boy can't breathe!"

Dr. Keiko Tamura raced out of the examining room, closely followed by her assistant. Sending Marco to call 911, she shoved the other kids on the bench over, picked up the choking boy and rested him face-down on her forearm, supporting his head with her palm. Then, with the heel of her other hand, she gave him three sharp slaps on the back.

"Ohmigod!" his mother screamed. "He's turning blue!"

Keiko turned the child over.

"Stand back!" she yelled to the women who were clustering around her.

"Give the doctor some room!" the boy's mother joined in.

Keiko gave firm, quick thrusts just beneath the sternum with her knuckles. No result.

"Please don't let him die!" The mother was in full panic now.

Keiko turned him over on his back again and gave three more sharp blows.

Marco hurried back to say, "They're on their way."

The boy had gone limp.

"He's fainted," Keiko said, expecting the mother would understand this was not the end.

"Ohmigod," she whimpered.

Keiko now administered mouth-to-mouth, squeezing the boy's chest between puffs.

On the fourth squeeze, he coughed and spit the piece of plastic out – and promptly started bawling, which under the circumstances was music that became a wailing duet as the siren of the approaching EMS unit grew to a crescendo, and it pulled up outside.

"Oh, thank God," the mother wept. She reached out for Keiko like a penitent trying to grasp the robe of a passing priest.

Eli strode in as the emergency crew was checking the boy's vitals.

Keiko recognized him from across the room. He walked over, and when he realized a crisis had passed, he pulled her aside.

"Still doing the work of ten men, I see."

Hers was a demure smile – much too sexy, he thought, to be appropriate for any clinician.

"Am I about to get lucky, or is somebody suing me?" she teased.

In all seriousness, he said, "I know I don't deserve it, but I really need your help."

THE CLINIC HAD A SMALL PLAYGROUND, and they took their conversation there. After he gave her a summary of what he knew so far, she said, "You don't know what you're up against."

"Oh, yeah, I do. I'm asking Coroner Sandoval's star pupil to call Danny a liar in open court."

Until a few months ago, Dr. Tamura had been deputy medical examiner to Dr. Martin Sandoval, who otherwise went by various media-awarded titles, including "Doctor Morbid." His long, pockmarked face and drooping eyes made him look like a Hollywood casting director's ideal choice for a ghoul who fed on fresh corpses.

"I started this clinic so I could get out of the department. And get away from him."

"I thought as much," Eli said. "You guys have a problem?"

"It was what HR would call a pattern of behavior, but there was one time it was beyond belief. And just my word against his. During an autopsy, he starts talking about the size of the guy's penis. He pauses the recording and wants to know, do I like them thick or long? In my ass or in my mouth? Now, you can imagine, the work is grim. You're used to it, but you have to find the jokes where you can. No intelligent, sensitive human being, no matter how professional, can be serious in that job all day, every day. He's making a joke. Everybody does. Or maybe he's coming onto me. Okay, maybe not everybody takes it that far, but it happens, and I laugh it off. But this time it's just the two of us down there in this high-tech cellar with only a roomful of stiffs as witnesses. What if he doesn't stop there? What if he decides to force himself on me?"

Eli asked her, "And I suppose, from a practical standpoint, reporting him wouldn't be an option?"

"Not if I want to keep my license in this county." Then she wanted to know, "Have you even *been* to an inquest?"

"Actually, no," Eli said. "But promise not to tell my client. It has to be a lot like a trial, after all. The coroner plays judge, only they call him the referee, and medical experts argue about what the autopsy results mean."

"He's not just the judge. He's also the star witness. He's the first one to explain his report, for the record." Here came the demure smile again, and she asked, "But who do you think is there to challenge him?"

"Besides us?"

"Who *should* be there?" she prompted him.

"That would be trial lawyers from the District Attorney's office," he supposed. "They'd have oversight authority to ensure due process. It's a legal proceeding, even if there's no specific finding of fault."

She shook her head. "That's the textbook answer. But in this town, the D-A will not go against the cops. Never. The attorneys might show up and log their attendance, but they don't participate. And the mayor, the city council? They don't want to know."

Eli was beginning to see that the politics of the case might easily outweigh the facts. "So, what's the check on the coroner?" he asked. "He could interpret the facts any which way, and as long as the cause of death is natural or suicide or clearly accidental, it's game over. Everybody goes home, the report goes in the file, and they call next of kin to have the body picked up."

"That's right," Keiko said. "As long as it's medically defensible – plausible, let's say – as long as the coroner raises no suspicion someone killed the guy – his report will stand as written. And if it involves the police, the file – containing the autopsy results *and* the entire inquest transcript – is sealed."

"Hypothetically, if the coroner was on your side, you could get away with murder."

"No, you're wrong about one thing."

"What's that?" he asked.

"It's not hypothetical. It happens all the time. It's routine down there."

Eli spread his hands like an auto dealer making a pitch. "How about it? You and me naked in the lion's den?"

"I seem to remember something about the naked part," she

said. If she worked that smile on him one more time, he'd forget his own name.

"I'm not the one who called it quits," he said softly, hoping it didn't sound like an accusation. Actually, he did think he was the one who finally decided to break it off. But he wasn't about to make an issue of it now.

She took a deep breath and let it out – either exasperated by their personal history or resolved to turn down his request. "Eli," she said and took his hand. "This case is a lost cause. It's a heartbreaker."

"In other words, you'll do it?"

8

L it from above by a glaring bank of purplish halogen
lights, Hank's corpse was finally under Sandoval's
knife. In that harsh light, the dark-chocolate skin looked gray
and ashen. He might be a mysterious, slain giant plucked
from a UFO, an elusive Bigfoot brought down, a Magic
Johnson in height and breadth of shoulders, but in the end,
he was simply a plain-speaking black man who had
committed the unpardonable sin of talking back to an angry
white cop.

Unlike the lonely hours the medical examiner had spent with
Keiko assisting him down here, this time Doctor Morbid was
surrounded by a grim-faced entourage. A microphone
dangled over the dissecting table from a junction box on the
ceiling above the spotlights. It was live, the tape reels were
rolling, and this time there would be no jokes.

Standing with Sandoval and looking on intently, as if in fear
the powerful man might suddenly spring back to life, were
Lt. Hughes, two police officers in their freshly pressed
uniforms, and several other youngish men and women in

those standard-issue gray suits worn by every bureaucrat on the planet.

Sandoval's tailored shirt and Italian silk tie peeked out from under his lab coat.

Into this huddled cabal, bursting through the push-bar double doors, came Eli Wolff, dressed in the better fitting of his two suits, a button-down shirt that used to be white, and the one pristine tie he owned. The suit, which was neat enough, was khaki. Walking in on the doctor's monochrome guests, Eli feared he looked like a delivery boy.

But he announced himself proudly. "Eli Wolff. Attorney for this man's widow."

Sandoval positively growled. "Counselor, you have no business here today."

Eli dared, "These clowns all have medical degrees?"

The doctor barked, "Get out of my examination room!"

When Eli stood his ground, Hughes snarled, "You *deaf?*"

Noticing the microphone, Eli raised his voice. "This man's family has no rights?"

Hughes' gave the barest twitch of his head, and the two officers started to move toward Eli.

But that's when Keiko walked in. Her high heels clicked smartly on the polished concrete. Her suit was navy blue, and her colorful scarf was Hermes. From the sheer class of her wardrobe and the confident way she carried herself, the onlookers who didn't know her might have assumed she was Sandoval's boss.

Shooting the question directly at Sandoval, Eli asked, "I believe you know Dr. Tamura?"

"Keiko," Sandoval said quietly. "You're his expert?"

"I'm here to observe on behalf of Mrs. Ellis," she said, with all courtesy. "With your kind permission, of course, sir." Eli caught the demure smile and was instantly jealous.

Sandoval blew out an exasperated breath. "Okay, Mr. Wolff." He spoke not to Eli but to the upraised scalpel in his hand. "You lucked out this time. She stays. You go."

And next time I'll just slit your throat, thought Eli as he swallowed hard, gave a side-wink to Keiko, and left the room.

THE CORONER's lab was housed in an unremarkable single-story building in an industrial district near the railyards. In the 1930s, the place had been a meat-packing plant, and its refrigerated lockers were economically repurposed to hold human corpses. The premises were perpetually damp and moldy, but none of the residents was in any condition to complain.

Behind a low masonry wall with wrought-iron fencing that separates the building from the road, there's a narrow lawn with a big shade tree. Eli had been sitting on a bench under that tree for hours. On leaving the autopsy room, he'd noted the time at 1:05 p.m. Keiko finally emerged from the front door long after dark, at 8:23.

He'd fallen asleep. She touched his shoulder.

"Let's have it," he said.

She shook her head as she led him out onto the sidewalk in silence. She walked briskly, and Eli noticed she was breathing hard. He was afraid she was having an anxiety attack, but then he realized she was probably just trying to get the stench of the lab out of her lungs.

When she stopped at the corner to wait for the traffic light, she looked up at him. That's when he saw her eyes were filled with tears.

"I imagined it would be bad. But… sometimes I'm not so proud to be a human being, you know?"

Sandoval's official statement made the evening news. On the live video feed from City Hall, he stood at a podium in front of the official seal. On one side of him stood Lt. Hughes and the suits from the autopsy room. On the other was Police Chief Harlan Nichols in full dress blues.

Sandoval did not look up as he read directly from the cover page of his report: "The cause of death was cardiac arrest during a physical altercation due to or as a consequence of arteriosclerotic heart disease."

In other words, the arteries of this poor, unfortunate man were so clogged from a steady diet of fast-food hamburgers and barbecue ribs that his chronic high blood pressure caused his heart to burst from the sheer surprise of seeing two well-intentioned cops come through his front door uninvited.

9

The halfway house was either halfway renovated or halfway tumbledown, depending on your point of view. A reformer like Eli might see an opportunity for development. A cynic like Vince would only find evidence of urban decay and the city's lack of commitment to social programs.

There being no available parking spaces on the street, Eli pulled into the gravel driveway on the side of the house. He pulled up behind a battered panel truck. He was worried he might be blocking it, then he saw it was jacked up on its left-rear axle. Missing a tire, the truck wouldn't be moving anytime soon.

He hadn't had a chance to get the Mustang's rear window replaced, so he'd removed it. He'd intended to duct-tape some plastic sheeting over it until he found time to go to a repair shop, but these days just finding time for that simple chore didn't seem possible. Now he had the fresh air of a convertible or a sunroof, which wasn't all that bad in the summer heat but brought a serious security concern. The coveted, collectible car would be an attractive theft target, especially with its new, flashy paint job and leatherette seats. For now, there was nothing to do but lock an anti-theft bar to the steering wheel and hope for the best.

Vince was standing on the wooden porch and called out, "You know, if anybody but an amateur decides to steal it, you'll be outa luck."

"And why is that?"

"Spray some air-conditioner coolant on the chromed part, and you can snap it like a twig."

Eli climbed the stairs to the porch and shook his friend's hand warmly. "So, is that the kind of practical advice you give these guys? Prepare them to go back out in the world?"

"I can't tell them anything," he said, then added, "and maybe neither can you. What's in the briefcase?"

"Writing paper and some cheap ballpoints. I figured you'd be short on supplies. Any last-minute advice before I try to work the room?"

He smiled. "Work the room? Yeah, it's like my girlfriend who tried standup comedy. Either they like you or they don't, and you'll know pretty quick. They won't have to tell you whether they want you back." Before they went inside, Vince turned to ask, "You still tracking with that hottie Miss Saigon?"

"She's Japanese-American, born in Denver. She's a doctor – a forensics expert – and sometimes the only way to get her hot is to talk about the physiological effects of blunt-force trauma. But the answer is yes and no. She's helping me with the case."

"Yeah," Vince said. "Usually I stick to the sports section. These days you got me reading hard news."

"Are you trying to say something?"

Vince's voice dropped as he said, "You should learn to pick your fights." And they went in.

VINCE GAVE ELI A QUICK TOUR. The structure was a Depression-era rooming house. It had four stories. Each of the upper floors had six bedrooms with a common wash-room, with a sink and toilet, at the end of the hall. Anyone wanting a shower had to book time in the one full bath on the first floor. Also on that floor was a good-sized kitchen with a pantry that had been retrofitted with industrial-grade stainless-steel sinks, worktables, and a door-type commercial dishwasher. There was a large dining room with floral wall-paper and an extended hardwood table. But even with a dozen bentwood chairs, there were so many residents they'd be eating in shifts. The comparatively small faux-wood paneled living room, which in the old days would have been called a *parlor* or a *sitting room*, was lined with bookcases. On the shelves were dog-eared paperback novels and an assort-ment of heavily-used school textbooks. Eli noticed there was algebra, English composition, world history, and – appro-priate but perhaps not consulted – *Problems of Democracy*.

Eli asked Vince whether he or some other staffer would be sitting in on the class.

What if they start pounding each other?

"Nope," Vince said. "I won't be far away. I got paperwork. You worried about a fight? Won't be one. These guys get out of line and it's back to jail. During the day, they're free to come and go. They can get all the body-slamming they want somewhere else. But if they leave the county, that's another violation gets them locked back up. No visitors allowed in here except social workers, medics, lawyers, and comic relief like you. Curfew is ten o'clock, and if any of them screw that up, getting locked out for the night would be the least of their problems."

The listless young men in Eli's class – there were nine of them – were seated around the table in the dining room. None were talking, not even among themselves. They were all dressed in freshly washed jeans and t-shirts. The shirts weren't uniforms or even all the same. They might have been thrift-store cast-offs, and some had team logos or school gym-program markings. Notably absent were gang colors or any headwear, including caps or bandanas. Haircuts were close-cropped, military style. Most of the guys were clean-shaven, except for one with a stubble beard and another with a neatly trimmed goatee. Most had some kind of tattoo on their fore-arms. Their ages were mixed, but they were mostly in their twenties and thirties. They were also varied in race, but mostly brown.

Stubble Beard (gray t-shirt, Abercrombie & Fitch) and Goatee (plain yellow) were both bald. Stubble Beard was the only white guy. He had Aryan Resistance tattoos on his neck and Swastikas on the backs of his fingers. Except for those two, Eli would remember them by their t-shirts. There was Mt. Kisco Athletics, Urban Outfitters, Warriors, My Mother Doesn't Love Me, Shawnee YMCA, Not Your Shirt, and This Is What a Feminist Looks Like. This last one was worn by a body-builder African American, and the faint smile on his face said if you teased him about his shirt, it would make his day.

Vince introduced Eli as an English instructor who would help them get ready for high-school equivalency exams. Their faces showed no enthusiasm for the opportunity.

As Eli passed out blank sheets of paper and the pens, he said, "My name is Eli Wolff and I'm here to help you do some writing."

Vince had advised him to ease into it. Eli thought he shouldn't play teacher and take roll, especially since attendance was voluntary. He didn't need to be a crack at math to figure the capacity of the house. With twin beds in each room, there should be thirty-six residents – maybe give or take a couple for overnight staff. Since he'd heard these programs always had a shortage of beds, most of his potential students must be elsewhere. He figured he'd learn names as they went along, as he engaged them in the work. He hoped the exercise would be a relatively painless ice-breaker. Plus, he'd find out who, if anyone, might have a genuine interest in learning to write better.

"Is this going to be some kind of exam?" Mt. Kisco, who might have been Jamaican, asked as he took the paper.

"Not at all," Eli said. "Call it an exercise, but it's really just a game where you use your imagination."

Look at their faces. Not the slightest interest.

"You probably know there are two main skillsets in the high-school exam. Those are math and writing. I suck at math, so I'm not your guy for that. But I do a lot of writing in my work. Many writers, including people like reporters who make a living doing it, say they sometimes get freaked out staring at a blank page. That's because you don't just write anything. You have to think first about what you want to say.

The job of writing is more about thinking clearly than it is about writing. Writing is just recording what you're thinking. Another way to look at it – writing is self-expression. Here you are staring at a blank page, and I'm going to tell you to write. And the question is – what are you thinking that's so important you'd want to write down? Of course, it's important if it's something you'd want to tell someone else."

Stares as blank as the pages in front of them.

"Okay," Eli said. "Here's the game. And it won't take long at all. There are no wrong answers. You're just going to write down whatever it is you decide to think about. Use your imagination. A teacher gave our class this assignment once, and it was amazing the things that came out of it. Here it is."

Eli tried to summon the glee of offering a kid a birthday cake. But they reacted as if he'd forgotten to light the candles. He pressed ahead anyway.

"Imagine a scene between two people. Could be you and a friend. Could be any two people – a man and a woman, two men, boys, anybody. It's up to you. But here are these two people. They know each other. You assume that they're friends, maybe relatives. And the thing is – one of them has a secret and refuses to tell the other one. Now, when I say 'start,' you're going to write for two minutes. Write whatever comes into your mind about those people – what they did, what they said. Write and keep writing. Don't take the pen off the paper. Don't worry about spelling or making corrections – just keep writing, whatever comes. Like I say, there are absolutely no wrong answers. You'll be amazed. Ready?"

None were ready because not one of them was holding his pen.

"Okay, humor me, and why don't you pick up your pens? The only rule is when I say 'start' you have to write. You have to write *something*."

The looks coming back to him were remarkably similar, as if to say, "You serious?"

Eli gave them his best and broadest grin. "I can't say 'start' until you all pick up your pens."

He found a way to get them to at least grab the pens. Like a waiter moving from one dinner guest to the other, he stood beside the Warrior and stared until the fellow grasped his pen. Then he moved to My Mother Doesn't Love me and stared him down until he held his pen. Eli deliberately avoided the feminist and was staring down at Urban Outfitters when the rest of them decided they'd go ahead and comply.

"Okay, *start!* Remember, *two minutes!*" And he studied the second-hand on his watch. "I want to see your pens moving," he said firmly.

His students exchanged exasperated looks, as if to say, "Is he serious?"

No one is starting. Bummer.

Eli thought about his recent transaction with Ramon and was surprised that he hadn't thought of the solution sooner. He pulled a twenty-dollar bill from his wallet and held it up.

Money talks!

"When I say 'start,' whoever gives me the most words on his paper by the time I say 'stop' after two minutes gets this twenty – no matter *what* you write. Now. Are. You. *Ready?*"

Their anticipation was an abrupt change in the temperature of the room. Every pen was suddenly erect.

"Start!"

Eli awarded the cash promptly to Goatee (in yellow), the one guy who asked him for a second sheet of paper. When Eli encouraged him to read what he wrote out loud, his response was, "It's kind of personal."

"Do you mind if I read it? Oh, and can I ask you your name?"

"No way, out loud. Not to these idiots," he said, handing over the two sheets. "And my name is Gabe."

Mock sneers all around, almost as if they'd had a meeting ahead of time and nominated this little guy to be Eli's star student. Maybe so the rest of them wouldn't have to do much at all.

Gabe was short and slight of build, with a complexion the color of cinnamon. A cholo. It sounded like English was his first language, but he spoke with a slight accent, almost singing the words like some coffee-house poet.

"Okay, Gabe," Eli said as he skimmed the first page, "fair enough. But unless you're keeping a diary, isn't the whole purpose of writing something down to share it? I mean, you know, communication?"

"Oh-ho, you didn't say nothing about that."

"Right," Eli admitted. "It wasn't part of the rules. I did say to write whatever came into your head. I can understand. This isn't therapy. Or confession." He handed the paper back to Gabe and announced to everyone, "This has been a way to get going. Get your thoughts flowing onto the paper. If you started out writing nonsense just to fill it up, I bet after a while maybe some actual thinking got done. Here's what I want you to do. I won't make you read these aloud, and I won't even read them. What you've got now we'll call a first draft. Now I'm going to give you some more paper, and we'll take the rest of this session – about fifteen minutes – and you'll write your second draft. This time, write it so you'd be willing to read it – aloud."

Vince stepped in at the back of the room and shot Eli a look that asked how things were going.

Having made sure each of his students had paper and with a nod to Vince, Eli went back to the head of the table and sat down. Emboldened by his progress so far, he said, "Oh, and this time, anyone who doesn't finish owes Vince five bucks or a turn washing pots in the kitchen."

On the second draft, compliance was pretty good. He got one sketch and another page full of expletives with what looked like prison or gang slogans, but the rest were honest attempts. The sketch was a competent rendering of a skull with a knife shoved into its crown. Eli guessed it was a copy of some tattoo. Someone should tell the artist that skulls don't bleed.

Gabe's essay was a story:

G had this girlfriend. She ran around on him. He didn't know for sure, but he thought that was so. He came home one day and she wouldn't talk at all. He asked her, "What's the matter?" It took her forever to say, "I'm pregnant." He wanted to know if it was his. She lit up mad as hell, screaming at him, "You got to ask me that?" He said, "Yeah, I got to ask." She ran out. Bitch is gone.

Remarkable. No spelling or grammar errors. Sentences so short and economical the thing could be an entry in the Bad Hemingway contest. It reminded Eli of the world's shortest novel, just six words, supposedly attributed to the Papa of modern English literature:

For sale – baby shoes. Never worn.

Gabe's story was hardly original. Eli could have guessed he'd get more than one essay describing hookups or breakups. Several others had to do with transactions gone wrong: A dealer counts the money and comes up short. Someone in the house drank the last of the milk and left the empty bottle in the fridge. A guy's friend offers to fix his car but drives off with it.

Those other stories weren't really stories at all. They were situations – like advertising those baby shoes. Something was wrong, and someone wasn't telling the truth about it, but there were no consequences. There was no second act – the twist payoff that the baby never got the chance to wear those shoes.

Now, Eli's goal wasn't to turn them into storytellers. But whether crafting fact or fiction, a writer should know how to describe a process. What were Eli's legal briefs but the process of logical argument? If he could get that skill across – whether it would be to tell a joke or dispute a parking ticket – he'd have done something worthwhile.

Gabe's story had a plot – a beginning, a middle, and an end. If it were fiction, it would be melodramatic. But Eli suspected the story was true. In that case, what impressed him was that it was the girlfriend who ran out. G stayed in the house. Did he wait for her return? And did he ever get an answer?

The amateur shrink in Eli further suspected that Gabe's story was the beginning of a confession. If he'd gotten that news, hadn't thrown her out, decided to stay in the house, and waited for her to return – perhaps he was prepared to be responsible. So, if she did return, how did he end up in jail? Did one problem situation lead to the other? Would it be racist to guess that he beat up the girlfriend and that's what got him arrested?

10

E li knew even less about Christian churches than he did about synagogues. He couldn't remember the last time he'd been inside of either. It must have been for some wedding or funeral. He knew that there were Catholics and Baptists. He seemed to remember that the Catholic iconography showed Christ on the cross but the Baptist's cross was bare – he didn't know why. President Jimmy Carter was a Baptist, he thought. There were conservatives called Fundamentalists, and Eli didn't know if they were a different group, but it seemed they were all over the news these days, raising their voices against abortion, gay rights, and the theory of evolution. Involvement in politics by these conservative whites in America seemed to be a fairly new thing, whereas Catholics had been steeped in politics for centuries – although, these days, it seemed they were more likely to be power brokers behind the scenes than the types who shouted on street corners. For example, Eli knew of three municipal court judges who were devout Catholics – two from Loyola of Chicago and one from Fordham in New York, both law schools that still emphasized their Jesuit roots.

When Bones invited him to speak at the A.M.E. church, Eli
didn't understand the significance of the invitation. It turned
out there were several A.M.E. churches within a few miles of
his house. The congregations were predominantly black. He
would later learn that the abbreviation A.M.E. stood for
African Methodist Episcopal, a denomination almost as old
as the Declaration of Independence and formed by black
Methodists back East who didn't feel welcome in white
congregations.

The significance was that A.M.E. churches traditionally
couldn't help but be political. Besides being places of
worship, they are grass-roots community organizations. And
that's not the only African-American denomination. There's
Christian Methodist Episcopal, Church of God in Christ,
and two factions of Baptists – National Baptist Convention
and the Progressive National Baptist Convention. Martin
Luther King Jr. had been a Progressive pastor.

That's not to say that these black churches were continually
fomenting revolution – quite the opposite. Historians will
record that, more often than not, these pastors were trying to
calm frayed nerves and quell righteous anger. And presumably,
that was the intent of Eli's appearance tonight. The rage in the
community over a string of "police-misconduct" incidents had
been simmering for years. And even though some of these
news stories made it to the back pages of the mainstream newspapers, they were recurring front-page headlines in the local
black-owned tabloids. The names of those victims were house-
hold words in the community, if not in the white suburbs.

When Lt. Hughes and Chief Nichols stood there on televi-
sion backing up Sandoval's announcement, it didn't take an
investigative reporter or an undercover cop to predict the

public outcry. The pot could boil over, and no person in a position of responsibility – no matter what ethnicity – wanted to see neighborhoods in flames. The large-scale urban riots of the 1960s were now a distant memory. The gang members who today controlled entire neighborhoods weren't even born yet.

Public anger was another factor Eli simply didn't consider. He'd been unaware of those stories in the community papers. He assumed that the cops were the enemies in this scenario, and he expected he'd be welcome at the church.

Bones would be driving his own car from the funeral home. They'd planned to meet on the church steps. As he had during his visit to the jail earlier today, Eli was cautious about where he parked. He found a place at the curb two blocks away and walked. He'd come directly from downtown, and he still hadn't had a chance to get the car window fixed. He worried about leaving his suitcase in the trunk. But he locked the club to the steering wheel and told himself he had more important things to worry about.

He didn't expect he'd be followed, but he was aware of the possibility. He resolved he'd be cautious and stay alert. On the way to the church, he thought through his speech. It shouldn't take long. He'd explain about the inquest, that it isn't a trial but a chance to be heard. And as the attorney for Hank's widow, he would make sure that the facts came out and went into the public record.

He met up with Bones on the steps of the church. The entry doors were propped open to relieve the summer heat, and the service had already started.

"That car of yours break down?" he asked.

"I parked some distance away," Eli explained. "Just being careful."

"We get you out in public, they don't dare touch you. Lighten up. And act like you got *good* news."

"I'm going to tell them we're doing everything we can."

"Oh, you gotta do better than that."

And they went in.

The congregation was singing "Shall We Gather at the River?" Every pew was filled, and people were standing in the aisles. The men were in shirtsleeves, the women in print cotton dresses. Some were in the uniforms of their trade. Most of them had come directly from work, probably without dinner. Even though the hymn's lyrics told of blissful peace in Heaven, their complaint was loud and defiant. They were used to singing together and in harmony. Many didn't even need to glance at the hymnals in their hands. Theirs was a voice, a force to be reckoned with.

Large ceiling fans spun slowly above them, like a flock of angels beating the air with their wings.

Bones led Eli up to the rostrum, where they sat down alongside two well-dressed African-Americans – state assemblywoman Violet Keyes and city councilman Mark Hathaway. He greeted their arrival with a polite smile, she with the briefest frown, presumably because they were late.

From his seat on the other side of the stage, Reverend Jeffords got up to take the pulpit. The congregation finished the last refrain of the hymn, and the people fortunate enough to be in the pews sat down.

An excited buzz went through the crowd, and Jeffords beckoned for quiet. "We must keep our wits about us here," he began.

Evans, an elderly man with a deep, resonant voice, rose from his seat and bellowed, "Our people are sick and tired! Tired of these coroners, these corrupt D-As, these all-white juries throwing their whitewash over this putrid mess they call a city government!"

A chorus of voices agreed with him.

"I'm sure we all feel that way, Brother Evans," Jeffords said with a cautionary gesture. "Now, will you please sit down?"

"I won't sit down!" Evans shot back. "I won't. I'm going to stand up forever!"

Applause now from the rest, and a few amens.

Then, one by one, a half-dozen also stood up as the first of them, Delores Cox, yelled, "Stand up for Hank Ellis! Stand up for justice!"

Voices chimed in, "For justice! Amen! For Hank! Oh, no, we're *not* sitting down!"

And then the entire congregation was on its feet, nodding their affirmations and shouting their anger in a collective roar.

Jeffords had to shout back as he raised both hands to push back, "You speak of justice, and behold our deliverer! I give you Luther Jackson, a pillar of our community, director of Jackson Brothers Mortuary, and a close personal friend of the Ellis family. *Please!* Show him some respect!"

Evans was the first to sit back down, slowly, as if he wasn't sure whether the pew had given way beneath him. And looking to him as if for approval, the congregation sat as if one body. The silence that followed descended as quickly as their anger had flared.

Jeffords announced, "Brother Jackson!" as Bones stood, beckoning Eli to follow. Giving a look of fearful encouragement, the Reverend stepped aside as Bones went up to the podium. Eli stood nervously behind him and to the side, hoping Bones would do most of the talking.

But Bones was brief and matter-of-fact: "Marcia Ellis asked for my advice. She has retained Eli Wolff, a very capable attorney and my good friend, to handle this matter. I give you Mr. Wolff." Then Bones motioned for Eli to step forward. To Bones' credit, he didn't sit back down but stood shoulder-to-shoulder with his friend, and Eli got the message. This was Eli's game to lose, but Bones would have his back.

The faces out there were sweating, and chests were still heaving from the emotional exertion. Eli began, perhaps not loudly enough, "It's very gratifying to see such a turnout for Hank."

From her seat, Mrs. Cox gripped the handbag in her lap and shouted, "Tell us what you're going to do for his widow! What are you going to do for those kids?"

He'd wanted to lead up to the explanation, but he found himself saying, "Well, first there will be an inquest. That's a medical hearing."

Perhaps thinking she was coming to his aid, Violet Keyes jumped up and moved between Eli and Bones to claim the edge of the podium. Hathaway was right behind her and took a flanking position on Eli's other side.

"Violet Keyes, State Assembly," she said curtly. "After an adamant letter from me and repeated phone calls by my staff, Coroner Sandoval has initiated this inquest –"

Hathaway broke in: "Mark Hathaway, City Council. I met personally with the mayor, and I have no doubt his efforts with the coroner were ultimately persuasive."

Eli finally raised his voice, "We're all where we need to be. We got action. The inquest is the necessary, the appropriate first step."

Evans shouted back, "Who is *we?*"

As if sensing Eli's boat might sink, Keyes and Hathaway quickly resumed their seats.

"Why," Eli said, "the family. And you – all of us who want justice for them and for the community. All of us who want to make sure this kind of thing can't happen again."

Evans was fuming as he rose again. "Can't happen? Won't happen? You think this is the first time? I'll give you some names – Eulia Love. Cedric Stewart. William Gavin. Cornelius Tatum."

"These were cases? If there are court records…"

"Yeah, cases – cases of mistaken identity. But nothing so significant as to wrinkle the brow of a single city official. Law-abiding citizens who are guilty of no other crime than *contempt of cop.* If that's a crime, then lock me up now. Lock us all up!"

"We're building a legal case, a lawsuit. Wrongful death against the city, on behalf of the Ellis family. We'll be seeking damages of five point one million dollars."

There was a pause out there while this fact sank in. Eli hoped they'd be impressed by his boldness, by the number. No such case had ever been won in this town. Not when the killers wore uniforms.

Then Dolores Cox demanded, "Is that what this is about, Mr. Wolff? Money?"

Lionel Davis wanted to know, "Are there no black attorneys in this town?"

Patrice Morehouse stood up. "Who do you think you are, mister? Come in here and tell us how it's going to be?"

This isn't going well.

Evans and Morehouse were still standing. Jeffords joined Eli and Bones at the podium. "My brothers and sisters!" he pleaded. "Mr. Wolff is a guest in the House of God! Please, please be seated and accord him the respect we wish for ourselves." Then he looked straight at the old man, saying, "Do unto others, Brother Evans?"

Evans nodded reluctantly and sat. Then so did Morehouse. Jeffords gave Eli a reassuring touch on the shoulder and returned to his seat. Bones leaned in, put his arm around Eli, and then he, too, sat down.

Standing alone center stage, a white guy in a sweaty khaki suit, Eli realized there was only one fact that could make a difference. "This inquest will have a jury," he said simply. "Probably mostly white. Be glad if they see me as one of them."

Then he looked straight at Evans and heard himself say, "Also be glad I'm a Jew."

Even Bones was surprised. Not that Eli was Jewish but that he thought this was the time and place to proclaim it.

"My grandfather watched as his parents were led into the ovens at Bergen-Belsen," he went on. "'Why are we the ones who lived?' he always wanted to know. As I was growing up, he'd ask me that question. As if a little boy would know what to say. I thought about it. Even after he was gone, I thought about it a lot. But here's the only answer that makes sense to me: We live so we can take responsibility."

"There's a new one." It came from Mrs. Cox. "How are you going to do that?"

"'Never again,' they told us." Eli kept his focus on Evans. "But you're right – *never again?* Who are we kidding?" He thought he saw the slightest nod from the old man. And something between a smirk and a smile. "They also say, 'You can't fight city hall.' But it must be a white joke because you do it every day. You've been doing it for generations. Me, I've fought rich corporations, big insurance companies, and their arrogant, high-priced lawyers. And I've won, more often than you'd expect. But I've never seen anything like this."

The faces out there were impassive. No one in this room would be willing to follow him anywhere. The tears that welled up in Eli caught him by surprise. He backed away from the microphone, shook his head, and rubbed his eyes with the heels of his hands. In that moment he lost his bravado, and, he feared, what was left of his courage.

His voice quavered as he stepped back up and said, "I'll be honest with you. I'm not sure I can pull this off. You've got no reason whatever to trust me."

There was a collective gasp, as if the organism of the congregation needed a gulp of oxygen. Bones shot Eli a look that seemed to question his sanity.

Then Eli remembered a phrase he'd heard when he'd flipped on his car radio early one Sunday morning. He'd caught the end of the "Gospel Hour" before he changed the station. He leaned into the mic and said in a low voice that he hoped sounded more humble than terrified, "I've heard it said, 'You pray for me, I'll pray for you. Because that's what God's people do.'"

He looked from Evans, to Dolores, to Lionel, to Patrice. "Please pray for me, and I'll fight for you. Because that's what God's people *have* to do."

Evans stared straight ahead. His eyes bulged as if he'd burst in another fit of rage. Then the old man shouted, "For *all* have sinned and come short of the glory of God!" And he brought his hands together in a single clap. And then another. And another.

The congregation joined him in applauding Eli, and they were all on their feet.

AFTER THE SERVICE, the Reverend led Eli and Bones outside ahead of the crowd. The three of them stood just outside the entry doors and shook hands with people as they left. Some said, "Thank you," others said, "Good luck," but most gave courteous nods or gripped his hand without a word.

Sirens were sounding in the distance, which was nothing unusual. But off in the direction where Eli had parked, there was a column of black smoke.

Eli and the minister seemed too preoccupied to notice. But seeing the smoke, Bones muttered to himself, "I've got a bad feeling about this."

When they were finally alone on the steps, Bones didn't remark on the smoke but suggested he drive Eli back to his car. "You'd best lay low. You're coming back to my place. Now."

"How'd I do?"

"They didn't throw you out" was all Bones would say.

ON THE SPOT where Eli had parked, what was left of the Mustang was a charred hulk. Firefighters were wrapping up after hosing it down, and steam poured off the hot metal.

Eli gave his details to a uniformed patrolman who acted as if torched autos were an everyday annoyance.

"Molotov cocktail," the cop explained. "Kind of a telegram. You owe money to some shark?"

"No," Eli said as he took his copy of the police report. "You want me to come in for questioning?" But the cop was already walking back to his patrol car.

"You can go home. We called for the tow, and they'll bill you," he said to his clipboard.

"Don't you care who did this?" Eli called after him.

The guy shrugged before he climbed in. "Damn shame. Sweet ride. Pay your bills and watch your back."

The loss included the suitcase Eli had packed for his stay with Bones. After the police drove off, Bones could tell that Eli was badly shaken by the experience. But all the undertaker said was "There's a bright side."

"Oh, yeah?"

"You get to replace those doofus clothes." Thumbing the khaki jacket Eli had on, Bones added, "And remind me to burn this one when you're not looking."

"You can burn it if we lose," Eli said. "Otherwise, it's my lucky suit, and I might never take it off."

"Yeah, look what it's got you so far."

11

Dear Lucille,

I really appreciate you taking the time to write me back. Having your letter and any news at all gives me hopeful thoughts when I have trouble sleeping, which is almost every night these days. Even then, I feel lucky when I grab few hours.

You suggested I should write to Brad, and that's just something I'll have to keep on the back burner. He was furious with me for sending him to you. It wasn't that he's so attached to me. He mostly didn't want to leave his friends. I can't imagine he'd miss his school. That place is such a dump.

Another reason is I want to step back and give him a chance to connect with Jack. I don't expect Jack to warm up to being a full-time father. Someday if things work out I want to be back in that role. For now, I can hope that Jack will be a friend to Brad, someone to talk to when he's confused or upset. I could write the boy, as you say, and give him all kinds of advice. But he wasn't that eager to hear it when he was with me, and anyway what makes me so damn smart?

The school sounds just great. I won't be too worried that Brad hasn't worked up any enthusiasm for his math homework. He got passing grades before, but I had to stay on his case to keep up with the assignments. That meant limiting the TV and time he wanted to spend hanging out with his friends. I'm surprised you say he's working on a science project. Wow, he wouldn't go anywhere near that stuff. Maybe his teacher lit a fire, or there's some girl he wants to impress? Yeah, I know, a young age to worry about what any girl thinks. But there has to be a reason. I'd love to know more about how it works out. Those kinds of projects and sports are the two things besides girls that can get a young man going.

The school seems well in hand, from what you say. Please keep me informed, but I'll try not to second-guess. I would appreciate if you would mail me his report cards. I leave it to you whether to tell him you're doing that. Like I say, for now as far as he's concerned I'm standing back.

One more thing I do want to mention, and I don't want to push, is his Christian education. I was never all that serious about being a Southern Baptist, and I was sure you got a lot more out of Sunday School than I did. I remember memorizing verses and the names of the books of the Bible. Then there were those "sword drills" where you tried to be the first one to turn to some verse they called out. None of that stuck for me, and it certainly didn't motivate me to keep going to church. I never took Brad, although I should have. I believe you told me Jack's family and especially his mother were Presbyterians. Did you go that way? If you're going to church regularly, I expect you'll take him along. That's all I'm wondering about – whether he's brought up with some kind of faith as a basis. When Clara passed, that was my biggest regret. I didn't even know who to call to arrange a service. More important for me, I don't have anywhere to go with my grief. I've tried to pray a few times, usually in the middle of the night. I remember how Rev. Paxton prayed, but the words don't come so easy to me. Also, I don't feel particularly worthy at this point to be bringing my case at all.

I've done things I regret. It's not so much that I got drunk and gave it to some loud-mouth. That's not the kind of thing I'd fret about. What bothers me is things it seems I have to do. It's not that they're wrong. It's what's needed to get the job done. They tell us all the time where the boundaries are, what it means to be a professional. But when you're out there, the world is all shades of gray. I try to do what's right, but I'm pretty sure that's not enough.

I see the check I sent you cleared, and I'm pleased about that. I'll be sure to send some more for his birthday, and I'll try to find a card with a thought that he won't think is too lame.

Once again, thanks with all my heart.

Your loving brother,

Bert

12

E li readily agreed that he should avoid returning home, at least until the perpetrators were found. However, the police apparently would be giving the incident about the same priority as a bicycle theft. Eli might as well count on being homeless for the duration of the inquest.

Bones lived in a one-bedroom bungalow behind the funeral parlor. The original plan was for Eli to take the couch in the living room. But midway through that first night, Eli's thunderous snoring got him evicted.

A groggy Bones led Eli next door and into a first-floor room. He flipped on the wall switch to reveal a display of burial caskets. The lids were open to show off the silk linings. There were wooden models finished in light and dark oak, cherry, and walnut. Steel-clad ones were available in white, black, and metallic gray, which looked to be high-quality automotive lacquer. Eli wondered idly whether Bones could order one for him in the same proud color he'd chosen for his ill-fated Mustang.

"Do I have to sleep in one of these?"

"Hell, no. You think I'd sell used merchandise?" Bones quipped.

"You said it was a spare room."

"Ain't nobody living here!" Bones flashed a smile, but Eli didn't appreciate the joke. "I'll get you a bedroll. You can spread out on the floor."

It was the sales showroom, with picture windows that looked out on the street. Eli was relieved to see that the heavy blue-velvet draperies were drawn. Then he realized it would be pitch black in here with the lights off.

"Who do you think did it?" Eli finally asked. "Who torched my car?"

"Could be the cops, warning you off. But also could be somebody who doesn't like you trying to be a person of color."

"What's that supposed to mean?"

"What was it all about at the church? They're supposed to get behind you because you're Jewish?"

"Well, I am."

"In this fight, you got to stand for something – all the way. No time for your usual bullshit. Blacks and Jews were tight for Bobby Kennedy. Not so much since. Don't assume."

"Are you saying I come across as a phony?"

"Eli," Bones said as he looked him in the eye, "you are the only white boy I know who sincerely wants to be black. And damned if I know why."

Eli yawned. "Because you're my best friend and I have more respect for your world than mine. Now, why don't you go find me that bedroll?"

~

BEFORE THE CAR-FIRE INCIDENT, Eli had set an appointment with Chief Nichols to get a deposition. It was to be mid-morning the day after Eli had moved in with Bones. Eli wondered whether the chief would acknowledge the crime, even though you'd expect he'd be aware. And if the cops didn't want to talk about it, fine. But if Eli could rub the chief's nose in it, why not?

Eli's change of clothes had gone up in smoke. There was no time to shop. The rumpled khaki suit would have to do. Bones offered to throw Eli's shirt and shorts in the wash, but Eli thought the dress shirt he'd worn last night looked a bit shabby for an up-close with the top cop. Bones had a closet-full of immaculate white shirts, but he explained that they were all slit up the back – that's how you fit them on corpses. He did have a nice assortment of conservative ties, and he encouraged Eli to pick out a couple as a first step toward classing up his court appearances. Bones also offered to run out and buy him new shirts, but Eli insisted he had a couple of good ones at home. Bones cautioned again that returning there might not be the best idea, but Eli persisted. Bones guessed it was an excuse. Eli needed to know whether his house was still standing.

Bones drove Eli over to a nearby car-rental agency, where they got a deal on a little red Chevette for less than a hundred bucks a week – about all Eli's insurance company would pay while they settled his total-damage claim. Eli just had time to drive by his house and, provided it was not a smoldering ruin, grab some clean clothes. Then he'd meet Bones downtown at police headquarters.

Eli phoned Keiko and told her about the skeptical reception he'd gotten at the church, along with the warm greeting someone had left in his car. She was concerned, but she didn't freak out. She, too, insisted on meeting the chief.

WHEN ELI PULLED up in front of his house, it looked even better than he'd left it. Ramon and Miguel had found his mower and gardening tools and were just finishing up the lawn work.

"Hola! Abogado!" Ramon cried out.

Eli was pleased, not only to see the neat yard but also that the boys were cheerfully making good on their promise. "Hey, Ramon! You guys are doing a helluva job."

Eli pulled a twenty from his wallet.

"You don't owe us nothing," Ramon said. "We're working it off like you said."

Eli pushed the bill at Ramon. "You need to watch my house for a few days. This is extra."

As Ramon took it eagerly, he nodded toward the Chevette, which he considered to be less than a real car. "You put the Mustang in the shop? For the window?"

"Nope," Eli sighed. "It's in the junkyard. Somebody damaged it a lot worse than you did."

"Sucks, man," Miguel said as he came over to see Ramon

shove the money in his jeans. "And you gotta drive that piece of shit?"

"What's your set of wheels, a skateboard?" Eli teased back.

"You gonna make them pay?" Ramon asked.

"You betcha," Eli said. Then he leaned in to task his new conspirators. "When I say watch the house, I mean watch the house. These guys who trashed my car are real creeps. Stay out of sight, and don't get close. You don't want to mess with them. I'll make sure you get some cash every time you give me a report."

He wrote the number of the funeral home on the back of two of his business cards and handed one to each of the boys.

"Somebody wreck the place, shouldn't we call the cops?" Ramon asked.

"Just call me. Especially if you see cops coming around when nobody called them."

"Miguel got no skateboard," Ramon giggled. "He don't even know how to ride one!"

"Shut up!" Miguel protested.

"You guys get in another fight, you'll be back to paying my lawyer fees," Eli said.

"No way!" Ramon yelled. "Do I got to give Miguel half?"

"Beats me," Eli said. "I charge for negotiations, so you guys better work it out on your own." And he went into the house.

~

Keiko was waiting for them in the lobby of police headquarters downtown. She had not yet checked in with the security guard. When Eli arrived, he pulled her back outside.

"I've been thinking about this," he said. "And my gut is telling me you should stay out of it, at this point."

"Off the case?"

"No, of course not. You'll still do the autopsy, testify, the whole plan."

"Then what's the matter with my going in there with you now?"

"Sandoval knows who you are. And I'm guessing he feels threatened by you. But you never met the chief, right?"

"No, that's why I –"

"You stay off his radar for now. You're a witness – probably the most important one – but you're not a co-conspirator. You're not on his enemies list, at least not yet."

"You think it was the cops who came after you?"

"I wouldn't be surprised."

"Thank God no one was hurt."

"I guess that was the idea. Send me a message – drop the case." Then Eli said to Bones as he walked up, "Bones thinks there are other possibilities."

"You know who did this to him?" she asked.

"Can't say that I do, for sure," said Bones. "Wouldn't put it past the cops. But could just as likely be somebody from our side."

"From *our side!*" she exclaimed.

"It could be all my fault," Bones admitted. "The brothers and sisters at the church were not too impressed that I brought in some white guy to handle this. And then Clarence Darrow here goes playing the race card – like they should trust him because he's a Jew. They're mostly not buying it."

"That's nonsense," said Keiko. "Where's your righteous anger?" she asked Eli. "You should be going to the press with this. Won't there be an investigation?"

"Either way, not a good idea," Eli said. "If it was somebody who wants justice for Hank, we'd be giving the police ammunition. And it could turn public opinion against the case. The cops are going to act like the brothers are going to burn down half the city if they don't stay tough. But, then, if it really was the cops, torching the car wouldn't have to be ordered from the top. They could have been rogue cops – buddies of the perpetrators, let's say – doing a little freelance work. Their supervisors might or might not know about it. If any senior officers do, they won't know details, and for sure they'll be looking the other way."

"I still don't understand what all this has to do with me," Keiko said. "You wanted me on the case, and I'm on it. And if we're talking stereotypes, one look at my face and Joe Average is going to think I'm qualified to be a medical expert. I'm anything but a liability to you now."

"I've got two reasons to see Nichols today," Eli explained. "The first is the reason I made the appointment – to get him to release Hank's body to us for an independent autopsy. He doesn't have to do that – not right away. He could come up with some excuse, stall us. He does that long enough, let's just say the evidence won't exactly be fresh."

"You have a point," she said.

"I'm not confronting him. I want him to think I'm a shyster going through the motions. Who else would be fool enough to fight City Hall? He has to assume it's a contingency case — but maybe I could just be in it for the publicity. Unscrupulous P-I lawyer just wants more slip-and-fall clients? I don't care what he thinks of me."

"Why does he go along with you?" Bones asked.

"I'm not saying we're suddenly best buds, but maybe I give him the idea this could all be over quickly if he just lets us do the examination."

"I suspect he'll see right through you," Keiko said. "What's your other reason?"

"The fire bomb. I want to see if he brings it up, not me. If it was rogue cops, possibly he really doesn't know. They wouldn't want him to know."

"Not much in this town he don't know," Bones said. "What happens if he goes along with giving us the body?"

"We do the autopsy right away." Eli asked Keiko, "Can you do it at the mortuary?"

"Sure," she said, looking at Bones. "I'm sure you've got all the pots and pans." Then she turned to Eli, "You and I, we didn't always get along. You've got this idea you're going to finesse Nichols. Well, good luck. I told you I'm in it, but for now keep me out of it. Don't get too creative, Eli. What we're after is evidence. And it will make our case, or it won't. What do you expect me to do now? I've got screaming babies back at the clinic, you know."

"Go home or go back to work, whatever," Eli said. "When they release the body, Bones will pick it up, and you can come over as soon as you can."

"Eli is staying at my place for the duration," Bones told her, "for obvious reasons. You're welcome, too."

"There's an underwhelming offer," she said.

"Think about it," Eli said. "It's not going to be party time, but I'd worry about you less."

"Call me at the clinic," she said. "If I don't hear from you, I'll check in before I go home." And she walked off.

As they watched her go, Bones said, "You can't keep *me* outta there."

NICHOLS GREETED them in his private office. Out of uniform, he wore a hound's-tooth sports jacket with suede patches at the elbows, gray gabardine trousers, a heather cashmere sweater-vest over a light-blue dress shirt, and an Ivy-League bowtie with rep stripes. He looked more like an English professor or a friendly shrink than the most powerful – and some would say, ruthless – man in the city, perhaps in the state.

The reception did not go in any way as Eli had expected. Nichols offered them a ready smile, a warm handshake, and fresh coffee. Eli declined the coffee, fearing that accepting the man's graciousness would be a step in the wrong direction. As they sat down in upholstered chairs, the chief began where Eli had expected to end. "Count yourself lucky," he assured Eli. "I don't think they meant to kill you."

"I wasn't sure you'd heard about it," Eli said.

"My department doesn't murder people, Mr. Wolff. Not even Hank Ellis. Whoever set fire to your automobile must not have wanted you to get hurt. But you can bet they wanted everyone to see." To Bones, he said, "Might there be people in the community who think he has no business taking this case?"

"I'm the one recommended him, sir," Bones said. "I've known Mrs. Ellis for some years, and she has asked my mortuary to render services at the appropriate time."

"Ah," Nichols said. "The arrangements." Still addressing Bones, he said, "Would you mind having a seat just outside, Mr. Jackson?"

Eli shot Bones a look, as if telling him to stay put, but his friend just said, "Certainly," and left the room.

"What is it my friend can't hear?" Eli asked Nichols when the door was closed. "Are you going to warn me off?"

"I'm doing no such thing, counselor. I just want you to be aware, as a responsible citizen, what is at stake here."

"I agree this case is significant. Although I suspect we'd have different opinions as to why."

"That part of the city is a war zone. Has been since before you were born. Race riots and gang warfare. We won't be having another national incident on my watch."

"Are you saying I'd be the cause of it?"

"It might not take much more than has happened already. You were lucky this time. We're all fortunate the damage was limited to your property. And let's hope the message was only meant for you."

"You seem pretty sure it wasn't your guys who sent it."

Nichols didn't think the question deserved an answer. "If Hank Ellis was killed accidentally, it's a departmental matter."

"Or a crime, if it was no accident."

"Either procedure was followed, or it wasn't. We have other, established procedures for dealing with those situations and taking corrective action. We've begun our investigation." He paused and then added, "If you want, we'll place you in protective custody."

"Oh, good. And I get your guys as bodyguards? No thanks."

"Mr. Wolff? You don't know who your friends are."

Again, the implication that the friends of my clients are my enemies.

Eli stood up. "Do you have a file on me?"

Nichols couldn't help smiling. "We do now."

In his mind, Eli said, *Put this in it!* and flipped the guy off. But he didn't. All he said was, "Figures," as he turned and left.

In the hallway, Bones rose to ask, "Well, do we get the body or not?"

Eli shrugged as he replied, "I didn't get a chance to ask."

"What was all that about playing the shyster, fooling him into thinking you were on his side?"

"You could tell it wasn't going that way."

"So much for your clever strategies. What do we do now?"

It didn't take Eli long to say, "The direct approach," and he led Bones back in to find Nichols in conference with Lt. Hughes.

"Mr. Wolff," Nichols said, "I was under the impression our business was concluded."

"Just one question."

"All right."

"Barricaded suspect. What's the procedure?"

"Call for backup and the hostage team. Evacuate the building and surround it. Try to talk him out."

"What you don't do, you don't go busting in there."

"That would be the textbook answer," Nichols replied.

Eli pressed it. "Was Hank Ellis killed with a choke hold?"

Nichols glanced at Hughes, sighed, and answered, "The choke hold has been barred by the Supreme Court. I presume you know that."

"On such a big man? As a last resort?"

Nichols took a long, deep breath as if summoning his last reserve of patience. "As a last resort, an officer would use his weapon – if he judged his life to be in danger. That's policy. And procedure. And in this situation, such was not the case. I would suppose, subject to confirmation at the inquest, that the officers did not deem it necessary to use lethal force."

"Then how come he's dead? I'm just trying to get a picture," Eli said.

Hughes stepped in to answer for Nichols, "A picture, Mr. Wolff? Our men reacted aggressively to subdue a dangerously disturbed man. For all they knew, everyone in that complex was armed and angry."

Nichols raised a cautionary hand to his lieutenant, and then in an even-tempered tone said, "Our officers acted bravely. We can't afford to discourage that kind of initiative, that kind of loyalty."

"We intend to conduct our own autopsy," Eli blurted out. Figuring they'd blown it, Bones shot him a look.

But then Nichols said calmly, "I'm sure Coroner Sandoval has done his usual thorough job. But you go right ahead."

HUGHES TOOK care of the paperwork, and Hank was at last a free man, for all the good it did him now that he was a corpse.

Keiko's car was in the drive when Bones pulled in with the hearse.

She came around to see him open the rear doors and grapple with the gurney.

"So, you, ah, live here?" she asked.

Bones flashed her a smile. "When I die, it's a short trip to the basement."

Eli, who had come out from the house, asked him, "I always wondered, do you have a problem asking your dates to stay over? I mean, when they find out you got stiffs in your closet?"

"You got your vampires, your zombies," Bones said. "My fine ladies don't have a problem with it. My job, I get respect around here. And mine aren't like the skanks you date – who are just grateful for the attention." He gestured toward the body bag on the gurney. "Meet Hank Ellis. I didn't know him. But he was the husband of a friend of mine."

"What's that about skanks?" Keiko asked Eli.

"Never mind," he muttered. "Bones makes shit up."

ELI HAD SEEN MORE than his share of dead bodies. There were those glossy photos of accident victims, along with some unpleasant viewings in the autopsy room. There were crime victims when he represented the survivors. And then there were the open-casket funerals of friends and relatives. Everybody has to deal with those. Mouths stitched into fake smiles and too many layers of pancake makeup. Eyeglasses, if the person wore them in life, to lend a touch of realism and familiarity. To observant Jews, the burial must be within three days, without embalming, so the caskets are typically closed and sealed. Doing it that way would be a blessing, in Eli's opinion. People think somehow it's a chance to say good-bye. Along with those resolutions the shrinks mistakenly call *closure*. But there is no closure. For the living, closure is a nicer word for *revenge*. And revenge is never as satisfying as you'd think. For memories of the dead, closure is pointless. The door is long since closed. The body, for which we have the descriptive term *remains,* holds none of the person who once inhabited it. The corpse is literally garbage.

Except when it's evidence.

And here was what was left of Hank Ellis. A giant. Graying chocolate flesh that had begun to putrefy. The smell was not quite enough to make you retch. Here was a man who should be singing and laughing and swearing and screwing. Instead of getting dissected – for the second time – in a feeble effort to find out how he gave it all up.

Eli, Bones, and Keiko had donned lab coats and surgical masks and latex gloves as they stood over Hank's body on the embalming table of the mortuary.

"This is unbelievable" was all Eli could say.

"Sandoval's report just says 'multiple contusions,'" Keiko said as she read from the accompanying paperwork. And then she called out the lesions as she found them so that it was all recorded on audiotape. Bones helped by using her SLR with its extreme closeup lens to take a flash photo of each area.

"Torso and arms, front view, seven bruises on the left arm. Ten on the right.

"Lower legs and feet, front view, six bruises on the left leg. Four on the right.

"Right side of the head, eye swollen shut, blood pooled in the socket.

"Left side of the head, gash beneath the eye."

Eli and Bones helped her turn him over.

"Torso and arms, back view. Twelve bruises, two open gashes.

"Backs of thighs. Left, four bruises, Right, six."

They turned him face-up again, and Keiko leaned over the body as she held a magnifying glass to study Hank's neck.

"Here it is. Contusion on the left side, sixty-degree angle to the vertical axis, about twenty centimeters long."

It was clear evidence of the application of a choke hold, the bruising difficult to see on black skin but indisputably there nonetheless. Caused by a baton being held in place against the carotid artery long enough to cause loss of consciousness.

Which is not long at all. One one-thousand. Two one-thousand. Not even time for a second thought.

Eli leaned back and sighed. "Which of these two cops decided to choke him, do you think? Oates, the hothead? Or maybe Torres does the math, knows they made a mistake going after this big guy, and he takes care of business?"

Keiko looked straight at Eli as she said, "Nichols wasn't worried we'd find this."

"Because?"

"Because he knows any competent medical examiner would see it. Especially if you were looking for evidence of a choke hold."

"What does that tell you?"

"It tells me the bastard thinks he has the case wired, and it doesn't make any difference what we find. It tells me the system is just as corrupt as we think it is. And our chances are effectively nil."

"Does this mean you don't like me anymore?" Eli asked her.

"I love you for trying," she said, in all seriousness. "And I'll do my part. But I think we should all understand what's at stake here. We'll make a statement, which will be in the public record – if they don't bury it. Probably nothing more. Very likely, nothing more."

"Are you done with this guy?" Bones asked. "Like my old man used to say, sooner or later it all goes in a box."

As Keiko was washing up, Eli stayed behind with Bones in the embalming room.

"I think it would be a good idea for Keiko to stay here with us, don't you?"

"Ask her," Eli shrugged.

"What was it with you guys?" Bones asked. "You got history?"

"You could say that. Somehow, I didn't live up to expectations. But I guess she's not letting it stand in the way."

"She can have my bed. I'll take the couch."

Eli was irked. "How was that not a possibility when it was just me moving in?"

"Give up my bed for you? Besides, casket room is a reality check for you. Me, I deal with it every day. I don't talk about it much. Who would want to hear? But I can't look at you – I can't look at anybody – without thinking about a writhing mass of stinking guts. Without knowing – which you might not appreciate – that your next breath could be your last. Now I got to suck the soft stuff out of this guy."

"Nice image," Eli said. "No wonder you're short of lady friends."

"We got summer sun," Bones grinned. "All picnics and lemonade. How could anything go wrong? But on those brightest of days, at the happiest of times, murders going down every second – *pop-pop-pop.*"

"You're jerking my chain," Eli said. "But what you're saying is, these cops have a tough job."

"The worst," Bones agreed.

"Maybe we just fold? Go home and lick our wounds? Bury the big guy and say some words from the Good Book?"

"Justice? We won't get it. But you have to keep demanding it."

"I got the feeling from Danny there could be another eyewitness," Eli said. "Do you think you can find him?"

"Like all us black dudes know each other?"

"Like I expect to be busy preparing the case, and, yes, you've got better connections in this community than anybody I know."

"I'll ask around," Bones said. "Now why don't you go get your jammies on? Trust me, you don't want to see this."

13

What was it about a graveyard? The concept itself bothered Eli. The Jews wanted you buried quickly – without embalming – as if to hasten your return to the earth. But then, if the purpose were to give back the resources you'd borrowed, a cemetery would be hardly the place to put them to productive use. The Christians, like the ancient Egyptians, wanted the body preserved in anticipation of a physical resurrection. It was a glorious destiny the old slave-masters thought only kings deserved. But the Christians apparently expected boatloads of believers to be ferried into the sky some bright morning. The Hindus, on the other hand, would not hesitate to burn you up before you stank. Despite beliefs about the soul's ascending with the smoke, the practice probably had more to do with land-use efficiency in India, where there was scarcely room to turn around, much less to reserve plots of land for planting generations of dead people.

And then there was that awful incantation, "Rest in peace." If there really is an afterlife, peace is the last thing Eli would want to find there. Heaven should be at least as interesting as here – or what's a heaven for?

In this city, with its sprawling millions, the notion of setting aside rapidly appreciating real estate as a shrine to loved ones seemed only a temporary luxury for the still-living. Perhaps for the span of the lives they had left, they'd have a few tearful visits from lovers, close friends, or dutiful relatives. Sooner or later the place would be a shopping mall or a high-rise or a retirement community. Considering the pace of population growth, immigration, and advances in healthcare, this urban metropolis will become the world's largest old folks' home.

Why prolong life if the result is only to give the person more time to stare into space? If century-long lifespans culminated in wisdom, you'd think we'd hear more about it. There are profits to be made in prolonging life, but not so much in ensuring the quality of that life.

Eli imagined that the work of Reverend Jeffords and his colleagues was an exception. Delivering an impassioned sermon on Sunday, however inspiring and necessary that may be, would not be the most important task of his busy week. Most of the hours in his long days would be taken up with visits to the sick and the dying. Quality of life – that's what he'd be selling.

Today, Eli stood at the head of Hank's grave and intoned the familiar comforts of The Lord's Prayer.

What else is there to do? Rage against the machine? Anger is natural and understandable, but there's no comfort in it.

Bones held Marcia's arm. She held little Lon's hand, and Lon held onto Janet's. Marcia was in the same dress she'd worn to their meeting, but the kids were picture-perfect in their new go-to-church clothes. Eli wondered whether the congregation had helped her pay for the new clothes.

Or perhaps she'd charged the purchases expecting Eli would be getting her some money.

He hoped she understood that it might take a while. And, thinking of his own debt load, he wondered what he was going to do about a car.

Eli recognized some of the faces. It seemed as though the whole congregation had turned out.

Off by a grove of trees, a man of medium height stood and watched. He was wearing a ball cap, windbreaker, and jeans.

"Who do you think that is?" Eli asked Bones as the mourners started to leave.

"Soon as we're gone, the gravediggers come in," he said.

"Those guys wear coveralls. Where's the backhoe?"

"Well, he doesn't have a camera, and let's hope he doesn't have a gun. I could say it's a free country, but you know it isn't."

BONES AGAIN WARNED Eli not to return home. But despite the car bombing and the quiet threat of the mysterious guy at the funeral, Eli was more anxious than he was afraid. He was less worried about bodily harm than someone trashing his home.

Then, too, Eli was never one to adapt easily to changes in his routine. Even though his wardrobe was limited, he disliked having to live out of a suitcase. And he found that stretching out on the floor of the casket showroom was not as creepy as it was uncomfortable. As a bachelor, he was not exactly an accomplished chef, but he had learned to cook for himself. Maria's Market in his neighborhood stocked the habanero chilies and the Pico Pica sauce he needed for his staple dish of beans and spiced-up Minute Rice. It wasn't that other stores didn't have the items. It was that Eli hated navigating different grocery shelving arrangements.

Eli dared to return to Maria's. He wore a hooded sweatshirt and jeans. He didn't own a ball cap, so he had to borrow one from Bones. As much as it pained Eli to wear a baseball hat bearing the insignia of a team he loathed, he needed it for disguise, which he completed with aviator sunglasses. He judged it would be more surreptitious to take the bus, especially since the color of the little Chevette was fire-engine red. But then he realized that checking on the house would mean he'd have to stroll through his neighborhood, and a quick drive-by would be safer.

He took the car and parked it a half-block and around the corner from the store. It didn't take him long to grab the half-dozen items on his list from the places where he knew they would be. Today, Maria wasn't at the register. A teenaged girl in a tight tank top checked him out. When he asked, he found out her name was Shelly, and she was Maria's daughter. He remarked to himself that so many second- and third-generation immigrants seemed to have WASPy given names. Was it truer for girls than for boys? When they married and took their husbands' surnames, they'd blend right in. It occurred to him that Keiko's parents had been the exception in naming her. Eli took it to be an indication of their traditionalism. He also noted that it must be no coincidence that thoughts of Keiko should flit by as he stood there trying not to stare at the shameless firmness of Shelly's braless breasts.

For a moment, he feared Maria might emerge suddenly from
the back and find him ogling the girl. Which, of course, he
was. And he hadn't acknowledged, until this moment, that
Keiko was back in his life, and not just as an expert witness.

"How come you like beaner food?" the girl asked him.

"I'm studying Spanish," he muttered. "Somehow I thought it
might help."

She didn't laugh but just stared back at him. It wasn't that she
didn't get the joke. Her look asked, *Is that the best you can do?*
This girl made him feel old. She was so young she didn't
understand that looking hot in this neighborhood might
bring her more grief than flirtation. But he wasn't going to
say anything. She wasn't about to take advice from some
lame gringo who didn't know better than to eat Mexican out
of a can.

Eli smiled at her, pocketed his change, pulled the cap down
further over his head, and left the store carrying his single
sack of groceries.

And who whizzed by on his skateboard just then but Ramon
with his backpack. It seemed like a coincidence, but later Eli
realized it probably wasn't.

"Hola! Abogado!" Ramon yelled, hopping off the board and
coming back toward him.

So much for the disguise.

"Well, if it isn't Ramon, my favorite client. You staying out of
trouble?"

Ramon dug into his pocket and brought out not one but two
twenty-dollar bills. "I met a guy pays better!"

"There you go," Eli said. "You washing cars now?"

He turned to walk away, but the boy grabbed him by the arm.

"He come by your house when we was working. He give me a message for you."

Eli looked around and instinctively pulled Ramon toward the protection of the alley.

"That so?"

Ramon laughed. "He says you sleep with dead people. What's that about?"

"It's not a joke," Eli said quietly. "He's saying he knows where I live now."

"You sleeping in some graveyard? That's sick."

Eli stood between him and the sidewalk. "What did this guy look like?"

"Just some guy. Maybe brown, maybe white with a tan. Dark hair. Maybe taller than you, but there's lotsa guys taller than you. Not fat. And he got money. Maybe he want to give you some."

"Clothes?"

"Nothing special. Like you."

"Ball cap?"

"Yeah."

"Did it say anything on the cap?"

"Not your team!" the boy giggled.

Eli offered to walk Ramon to the bus stop and wait there with him, but the boy took off on his skateboard.

Eli decided to skip the drive-by this time.

ELI WAS PUTTING his groceries away in the pantry at Bones' place when his friend came charging into the kitchen.

"Where you been? I think I know where Danny is."

Eli shushed him and led him out into the driveway.

"What's up with this?" Bones demanded. "I have stuff to tell you."

In a quiet tone, calm as he could manage, Eli said, "They know I'm here. And you have to figure they're listening to our calls."

"How do you figure?"

"Kid from my neighborhood followed me to the store. They're sending messages through him. I think it's Torres."

"The young cop? Trying to warn you or some shit?"

"I think it was him at the funeral. Unless it was one of Nichols' spies."

"You getting any sleep? If real spies follow you, you won't know it. It wouldn't be Torres, and they don't be sending you no messages."

"Are you telling me not to worry?"

He laughed. "You? You get paid to worry. We can't have you going broke."

"You found Danny?"

"Could be. Got a tip," Bones said, indicating the Chevette. "We better take your rental. Nobody be looking for me in no kiddie car."

Bones went to get into the driver's side, and Eli shot him a look. Bones stretched out his hand for the keys. "Don't be looking at me that way. You got bad car karma. I still got *my* ride."

~

BONES PULLED up in front of a rundown house on a slum street. Dirty and crumbling stucco, bars on the door and windows. Dead grass and dirt in the front yard, along with a rusted barbecue and some old tires.

Bones started to get out.

"Are you planning on just marching in there?" Eli asked.

"You got a better idea?"

"But he doesn't know you."

"And his peeps in there, whoever they are, they don't know *you*. You head for that door, and they're gonna think you're somebody's parole officer."

"How are you going to get him out if he's in there?"

"Offer to buy him a meal. You said it worked before."

"He just might go for that," Eli agreed, and Bones went up to the door.

It opened a crack at his knock. It was on a chain. After a

short conversation, Bones returned to the car and motioned for Eli to get out.

"They said he took off this morning. Let's have a look around."

Bones explained as they walked into the alley behind the house. "If a car didn't pick him up, then he's walking through the neighborhood. If he's strung out, he's got no plan. Just doesn't want to stay anyplace for very long. He must be living like some homeless guy, which is actually not a bad cover. He's hanging out in doorways, trying to stay out of sight. Most of all, he's scared."

"He has that girlfriend, Cyndi."

"From what you told me, he's gonna be staying far away from her. He's not going back to her anytime soon because he's afraid he'd be leading them to her. If she's a witness, they want her as bad as they want him."

They found him three blocks away in a dumpster. The body was cold, but the blood was still wet.

14

E li and Bones were filing a police report at the stationhouse when who showed up but Lt. Delbert Hughes. Hughes had a look at the paperwork then summoned Eli into a private office. Bones found a chair and waited nervously outside.

They both sat, and after a few moments of cold silence, Hughes said, "Kind of a coincidence you finding this guy."

"Why wouldn't I be looking for him?"

"Why would it be so easy to find him would be my question."

"Mr. Jackson was a childhood friend of Hank's widow – you know, my client? And Danny was Hank's cousin. That's like one degree of separation. And my friend has friends on the street. It's a small town, down there in the 'hood."

"We will have to know who those friends are."

"I'm sure he'll be happy to cooperate if you'd just invite him in."

"Look," Hughes said, "however you found the victim, it's pretty obvious you came on a dope deal gone wrong. Person or persons unknown. We've got our sources, and we'll try to run it down, but I don't see much point in this going further."

"Person or persons unknown bombed my car. And Danny was a material witness in my case. Do we just say, crazy shit happens?"

"Mr. Wolff, I got a crack-head corpse in a garbage bin where he belongs, and the only two suspects for miles around are you and a pimp with an attitude who says he almost played pro ball. Now we might have a hard time convincing a jury you could work yourself up to this kind of thing, but I could easily like your guy Luther for this. Now, how far do you want me to go?"

"You're attempting to intimidate me by threatening Mr. Jackson with false prosecution?"

"Do you know Mr. Jackson didn't do it? You said he was the one who found the body. And you said he drove right to the house where the victim was last seen alive. It seems he knew right where to look. And his friendship with you or even his connection to Mrs. Ellis might not have anything to do with anything."

"He was there only because he was helping me. And I was right behind him when he found the body. Your imagination is going all the wrong way."

"We have officers on that beat who might say otherwise. You see my problem."

"What do you want from me?" Eli asked.

"I've been in homicide sixteen years. I've seen a thousand cases like this, and they all defy investigation. A couple of years from now, some prisoner brags to his cellmate he did this and some others. The story comes out sooner or later, but it's not exactly headline news."

Hughes got up and stood over him. He looked as though he was going to deliver a lecture, but then he must have thought better of it. He relaxed and sat on the edge of the desk, slapping his thigh nervously with the case file folder. His voice softened. "Oates and Torres are righteous guys. They'll testify to the sequence of events, nothing you don't know already. But if you try to trip them up, you know they'll take the fifth. When all is said and done, what have you got? We don't have to be enemies here."

"We want the same thing," Eli said, and he thought he saw Hughes start to smile. "We want a city where people respect each other, where they do their jobs and pay their taxes. And send their kids to school instead of to some funeral home."

"That we do," Hughes agreed.

"But we probably disagree on who gets to decide who to kill to get that done."

Hughes didn't prevent Eli from getting up and walking out.

As they left the station, he told Bones, "If I'd looked at him the wrong way, they could have held you on suspicion of murder."

"You told them – what? – that I have a conflict in my calendar?"

"They're thinking I'm going to drop the case."

"Eli Wolff? The Jack Russell Terrier of jurisprudence?"

"I'm thinking – if it's Torres sending messages, maybe he doesn't mean to threaten me. Maybe he's trying to warn me."

"That would be giving the guy a lot of credit."

"One of those guys choked Hank to death. The other one let him do it. If it's possible to have a chat with Torres, I say we try."

THIS TIME the information came from Eli's network of spies. A private investigator he'd sometimes used on accident investigations steered them to a sports bar where cops were known to hang out after hours. The detective was even able to tell them the shift-change rotation so that they'd be able to time their visit when they'd be most likely to find their man stopping in on his way home.

Before they entered the bar, Bones said to Eli, "I know this is gonna be hard for you, but we get into a spot, let me do the talking."

"If there's a fight, you can handle that, too," Eli quipped, but Bones didn't find it funny.

Inside, as if taking command right away, Bones signaled the bartender to draw two beers. The small bar was crowded. There was no one in uniform and no women.

"See him?" Bones asked as Eli looked around.

And, sure enough, there stood Torres in the back chalking his pool cue.

"Pool table," Eli said.

"Not my game," Bones said. "His buddy around?"

"Don't see him."

"Well, then," Bones said, "oblige the man. I won't let you hang, but if I do see the big guy, I'll be the first one out the door."

Eli strolled over to the wall rack, selected a cue, and approached Torres.

"Friendly game of eight-ball?" Eli asked.

"Friend or foe isn't the question," Torres said, not at all surprised.

Eli racked them up, then rolled the cue ball across the table toward the cop.

"You break," Eli said.

Torres assumed his stance, curled his fingers expertly around the cue, and took his shot, a precise tap that caused the four ball to nudge the rail. The four wasn't an easy shot, and the rest of the balls were still nestled in a tight cluster with no clear target.

"You sure don't leave me much," Eli said.

"Do you even understand the game?"

Eli studied his shot for the briefest moment and then slammed the cue ball recklessly, which caromed off the nine ball and disappeared in the side pocket.

"Off to a hell of a start," Eli grinned. He knew enough to know that scratching the cue ball had lost him the game.

"You are so bad," Torres said, "this has got to be a hustle."

Eli reached into the return for the cue ball and came close to Torres as he handed it over.

"I saw you at the funeral," Eli said in a low voice.

"No, you didn't" was the quick reply. But the cop didn't ask which funeral, nor did he pretend not to recognize Eli.

"Did you know Danny Ellis was murdered today?"

As Eli turned to study the table, he didn't see Oates come up behind him.

"You didn't think they'd do it, did you?" Eli continued without looking up. "We need to talk. And I don't mean by skateboard telegram."

Bones got there a second too late holding two beers. As Eli turned to take his, he saw Oates at his elbow. The senior cop took both beers from the guys and set them on the table.

Indicating the back door, Oates said, "Step into my office?"

"Love to stay and chat," Bones said, trying to move away, "but …"

"This won't take long," Oates said as he pushed them toward the door.

Torres followed them out. The afternoon sun was blinding, and Eli noticed uncomfortably that there was nothing in the alley but an open dumpster.

Oates moved toward him. Eli was sure a fistfight was coming, but he hoped he'd fake them with, "Tell me, which of you killed Danny?"

"Damned if I know," Oates said. "Wrong place, wrong time. Worthless piece of shit, but don't quote me." He didn't raise his fists, didn't make any sudden movements. But he came very close and said softly, "Look, let's just leave the kid out of this."

Well, this is unexpected.

"The kid? You mean little Ramon?"

"The kid doesn't know anything. Leave him out of it." Yes, of all things, Oates seemed worried about protecting Ramon.

From what?

"Are we talkin' about the same kid?" Bones asked.

"My guy?" Eli asked. "The one you use to send me threats?"

"No one has threatened you," Oates was quick to say. "But you should take some advice. Like, use sunblock. Wear a condom. Fuck off before you get yourself fucked."

And with that, Oates nodded to Torres, and they both went back inside.

Eli and Bones didn't dare go back in. Those guys had done all the talking they were going to do.

"What was that about?" Bones wanted to know. "We shoulda got our asses kicked."

"And why is he so worried about Ramon?" Eli was still trying to figure the connection. "It's like they're trying to put us on the defensive. As if we're not already, you know? Like somehow they think we've got something on them. Not just a winnable case – but something new. Something about Ramon?"

"I don't understand what the kid has to do with it. You're the only one of us knows him."

"Yeah, until they go sneaking around my house and give him forty bucks to deliver that message."

15

Eli phoned Vince. "It might be a good idea for me to skip a few classes," the lawyer said. "At least until this case is over."

"You wimping out?"

"Just trying to be safe."

"Let me clue you to something, my man. I'm employed by the sheriff's department. I'm an officer of the law. I got a badge and a gun. Actually, several guns. I fear for my life every day. Now, if I get especially scared, I can't go to my supervisor and ask for a desk job until it all blows over. That's what they do when they think *you've* done something wrong and they need time to figure out whether you get to keep your job."

"So you want me to come down there? They firebombed my car, you know."

"That's right. My Chicanos all drive Chevys. No doubt they had something against your stinking Ford. Whether you give a class is totally optional and won't make the slightest difference in the history of the world. I was trying to do you a favor because it seems like you need more reasons to get up in the morning."

Do I look like such a sad case?

"I'm not saying I didn't like doing it."

"Drop by anyway. There's a guy wants to have a talk with you."

"Grammar question or legal advice?"

"No idea. Your new best friend Gabe keeps asking me when you're coming back."

Vince left Eli with Gabe in his second-floor dorm room. There were no chairs, so they sat on the edges of the twin beds and faced each other. Eli had his briefcase, this time with a yellow pad in case he needed to take notes.

As Vince closed the door on the way out, he quipped, "Now you two behave. Both feet on the floor, and keep your pants on."

"His girlfriend's a comedian," Eli said to Gabe when Vince had gone.

"Old news," Gabe said. "She took a hike on him a while ago."

"Oh, yeah?" Eli took a chance when he said, "I guess you know what that feels like."

"My story, you mean?"

"Yeah. Didn't seem like the kind of thing you'd make up, you know, if you had a choice."

Gabe dropped his head and stared at the floor.

"I'm sorry," Eli said. "Vince said you wanted to talk. He probably told you I practice law. Emphasis on the *practice*," and he forced a chuckle. "You worried about something?"

"I guess I got to step up."

"How's that?"

"It was me and Pilar. Three years ago. True story."

"I figured. She ever come back?"

"Oh, yeah. Two days later. Where's she gonna go? The other guy wasn't about to keep her if she told him she was having a kid."

"So you knew there was another guy?"

"It wasn't like she was sleeping around. Not that she wouldn't ever, but I knew the situation. There was this one stinking, big-ass vato. She worked for him. He had this housecleaning service. She ran the crews. They'd send a team of maybe two or three into a place, be done in a couple hours. So a team does maybe five houses in a long day, and they got six teams. That's a lot of houses."

"Sounds like a good business."

"As legit, it would be sweet. But the boss is hooked up with a gang. The whole operation is in on it. The crews know when somebody's going to be on vacation, when a house is empty. They tip the gang, and those guys rip the place off."

"How does that work? It wouldn't take a genius detective to figure the connection to the cleaning crews."

"They're smart and they're careful. They never hit their own customers. They're keeping their eyes open for newspapers or mail piling up at the neighbors. Cars that don't move from parking spaces."

"Even then, it doesn't seem like they could get away with anything for long."

"The cops are in on it."

"Paid off?"

"Not just that. They got safe houses all over town where they stash the goods. Cops fence the merchandise with their connections. Everybody splits the take. Every now and then they run some homeless guy in for a burglary, and he's released in no time for lack of evidence."

"Is this what you wanted to tell me?"

"For what? What do I care? And what could me or you do about it if I did?"

"Back to your girlfriend, Pilar. What happened? You beat her up? Is that what put you in jail?"

"You got a high opinion of Chicanos."

"You took the rap for something."

"I went after her pusher with a kitchen knife."

"I see. So, she had a habit?"

"Not right away. She starts showing, the boss wants her nowhere around. She's out of a job. She's living with me. I'm working in an auto parts store. It's okay. I'm not getting rich, but I make the rent and we eat. She's clean at that point. Now, she got no family. No sister, no mother, nobody to help. The neighbor knows a midwife, and Pilar has the baby at home. She can't deal with it. I'm working the job. She tries to get the neighbor to help, but the bitch stresses out, says it's too much and makes a call to family services. The social worker shows up a few times, then they take the baby, put it in foster care. Pilar is wrecked, reaches out to the vato, gets connected to crystal meth, and before I even know she's using, I come home, and she's dead in the bathroom."

"You had no idea she was using? How did she pay for it? And couldn't you tell she was strung out?"

"She didn't get money from me. I didn't trust her with it, and I even made the runs to the grocery store. No, I guess she was sucking off the vato. The pusher was a guy on one of the crews. She'd stay away for days at a time. At first I didn't think about the drugs. She lost a lot of weight, and she wouldn't go to the doctor. She wouldn't eat much, and so I thought she was sick."

"So you got arrested for assault with a deadly weapon? Did you tell all this to your public defender? To the judge?"

"Not all of it. No way was I going to name the vato or tell them his business. That would be like a death sentence, you know? They'd hunt me down. But, yeah, the whole sad story helped. Convinced them I'm not a violent criminal. That's how I ended up here for my parole instead of locked up forever."

"You still haven't told me how I can help."

"The baby's name is Marco. He'll be two next week. If he's still in foster care, if he didn't get adopted already, when I get out, I want him with me. When I was on the inside, I connected with my sister in Veracruz. We'll find a way."

"So you found out he's yours?"

Gabe shrugged and said, "A guy's got to step up."

"Nobody in family services stayed in touch with you?"

"Are you kidding? I'm the last guy they're going to tell about anything. I got no idea where he's at."

Eli took the pad out of his case and started to make notes. He got Gabe's name and personal details, any data that could help trace baby Marco in the system.

"This shouldn't be too hard," Eli said. "And if I'm making the inquiries, the doors might open easier."

"I can't pay for this," Gabe said simply.

So what else is new?

"I'm not expecting it will take a lot of my time to find your son. What happens next, it's too early to tell. All I can promise is I'll try to hook you up with people who can help. People inside the system who mostly need to be talked into doing their jobs."

"I'd be lying if I said I had it all figured out. But I got to start somewhere," Gabe said.

Worrying about Ramon is what got me into this.

"Maybe you can tell me something," Eli suggested.

"If I can, sure."

"What do you know about little kids getting used as messengers? Or as mules?"

"All the time," Gabe said. "But it depends on the situation. If it's a gang moving stuff around, it's going to be some kid already in or wanting in. Somebody who's been initiated. Like, he's fourteen."

"What about the cops?"

"They're not moving drugs. They want to stay out of the action. But they'll use a kid to carry cash. I mean, he don't have a driver's license. He's getting around on a skateboard, a bike, or a bus. So zero chance of a traffic stop, and he's not even in the system. And what's so suspicious about a kid with a backpack?"

Gabe said he would be up for release in a month. Eli promised to get back to him before then with any information he could find on Marco's whereabouts.

16

Eli, Keiko, and Bones sat in his kitchen eating Chinese takeout from paper cartons. Eli was struggling with his chopsticks, while Keiko and Bones were using their plastic forks.

"Did you buy this because of me?" Keiko asked Bones. "My people were Japanese, not Chinese."

"The place is a block away," he explained. "There's a drive-through."

"Besides, Moo Goo Gai Pan is big in the 'hood," Eli added.

"Like you would know?" Bones came back. "How come you're eating the shrimp? I thought that stuff was off the program."

"I don't eat bacon because a pig is a sentient being and I don't want to get my arteries clogged. My dietary choices have nothing to do with my being Jewish."

Keiko got serious. "What were you guys thinking? They could have killed you both right there."

"Sending the kid to warn you off, okay," Bones said. "But killing a witness? That's fearless cold."

"I still think Torres is the guy with a conscience," Eli said. "Maybe Oates finds out Torres is trying to start a conversation – through the kid – and he's going to put a stop to it. If Ramon is the link, Oates doesn't want any more messages getting passed. That must be why he says lay off the kid."

Bones asked Eli, "What makes you think Torres is so righteous? Just because you saw him at the funeral?"

"Eli," Keiko said, "I told you this case was pointless from the start. And if they're going to go hunting down anyone who saw anything …"

"They're rogue cops," Bones agreed. "Killers. But they don't think they're outside the system. They think guys like Hughes have their backs. What's to stop them from doing anything?"

"These cops may be killer types, or not," Keiko said. "I'm thinking they got themselves into a bad situation and had to do what they did to make it out alive. But the department does stand with them. And those two guys aren't necessarily the ones you have to worry about."

"Who else?" Eli asked her.

"The department has a surveillance division," she said. "It's supposed to be anti-terrorist, but that's just what gets them funding. Do you remember what's-his-name, dropped out of the Senate race?"

"Patterson," Eli said. "Heart problems."

"The Chief's spies followed him to Acapulco, got them on video. His heart problem was he forgot to take his wife."

"What does the U.S. Senate race have to do with local cops?"

"It's a high-profile lesson. Bringing the guy down showed they can do it to anybody. And messing with the Feds gets them respect all up and down the line. It doesn't mean the Chief won't pay attention when the DOJ calls, but it does mean they try to let him run his own town."

Eli was impressed. "The chief of police has that much power?"

"This city and not many others stood up to the Mob. The Feds hate those guys," she said.

"Let's get real, here," Bones said. "The cops may have some serious weight behind them, and I'm not saying there's no call to be scared. But once the hearing starts and we show up in court, it'd be pretty bad publicity if any of us showed up dead."

"There's another consideration," Keiko said. "There's been so much publicity, the department has to hold the inquest. And if they think they'll win, they want it. Eli, you and I are expendable. A lawyer and an expert witness – it's not like we're the only ones who could pull it off. I doubt they think that taking us out of the picture would make any difference. Not if they have the whole process rigged. And, Luther, you don't have any special knowledge of the case. No, Danny was an eyewitness, maybe the only one. And he would have been a problem for them."

"I still want to talk to Cyndi," Eli said. "And the best way for her to stay alive, as you say, would be to take the witness stand."

"Sad to say," Bones said, "whether Danny knew it or not, he died to protect her. I'll see what I can find out."

~

THE NEXT TEN days were spent in preparation for the hearing. While Bones asked around as discreetly as he dared about Cyndi's whereabouts, Eli regularly took the bus to the public library, where he pored over medical texts and made notes. Keiko had an anatomical chart she'd brought from her office, and in the evenings she quizzed Eli on the relevant body parts and terminology.

Eli also transcribed Keiko's autopsy notes from the tape recording, typing it himself on the Selectric in the mortuary office for fear that some hired secretary might sell it to the newspapers or the cops. He highlighted portions, made careful notes in the margins, and used a scheme of index numbers to correlate portions with his presentation brief.

The whole process reminded Eli of cramming for final exams. When he stretched out in the casket room at night, he craved sleep, but his mind was still racing. When he finally did drift off, he had fitful dreams of walking into the exam and realizing he'd studied the wrong textbook or finding out right before graduation that he hadn't earned enough credits for a diploma.

Keiko agreed she shouldn't go near the clinic, but she declined the offer to shack up with Bones and Eli, whom she sometimes referred to as "the odd couple." She preferred to stay with her grandmother in their bungalow in a middleclass neighborhood. As Sandoval's former deputy, she might be his worst-nightmare opponent in court, but she felt her visibility put her out of range of physical threats. This didn't stop her worrying about Eli, and not just because of possible reprisals from the cops, but also because the African-American community was not a hundred-percent sold on his representing them.

In the days preceding the hearing, she stopped by Bones' house often. Whenever she was there, she couldn't help taking time every couple of hours to phone the clinic. She was stressed about not being able to see her patients. As for the case, she knew her material cold and left Eli to work through his notes and hers. She got so bored she willingly undertook light housekeeping and even some cooking chores. Anything to avoid pizza and Moo Goo Gai Pan. She even catered to Eli's preferences by concocting vegetable casseroles and stews, and he was secretly happy to keep his supply of beans and habaneros in their cans.

The day before the hearing, Bones still had no further information on Cyndi. In the afternoon, he suggested that he and Eli go over to school playground to get the kinks out by shooting some hoops.

In a game of one-on-one, Eli furiously dribbled circles around Bones, who had only to pivot and extend a long arm to block most shots. The taller man held his right arm behind his back to even the odds.

Eli finally turned abruptly, hooked a long one toward the basket, and scored with a swish. Bones reached up and palmed the ball before it bounced.

Eli asked, "Did you let me do that?"

"You fly so low," Bones replied with a sly smile, "my radar don't go that far." As they walked toward their towels, Bones grabbed him behind the neck. "Eli, my brother, I'm real sorry I got you involved in this. You ready for tomorrow?"

"Ever seen a possum?"

"Quite frequently," Bones said. "They go after my garbage. Nasty critters."

"They get fat, stubborn, and mean," Eli said. "Teeth like razors. Fight to the death." He buried his face in the towel and took a deep breath. "I saw a little terrier kill a possum once. Twice its size. Blink of an eye, went for its chest. Chewed its heart out."

THAT EVENING, Eli drove to the cemetery. At Hank's grave, he found a freshly carved granite headstone. He knelt to trace the inscription with his finger:

HENRY ELLIS
JULY 16, 1952 – SEPTEMBER 4, 1981
IN LOVING MEMORY
YOUR FRIENDS VOW
'NEVER AGAIN.'

Just then, Eli sensed that someone was standing right behind him.

Not now! Why didn't you kill me before I put in all that work?

Eli rose slowly and turned – to see old Evans standing there in the moonlight with his hands clasped in front of him.

"Mr. Evans. Do you know the hearing is tomorrow?"

"I do know," he said. "I come to say a prayer. I be there."

"In Jewish tradition, we wait a year to put up the headstone. I was surprised to see this."

"A year is a long time," the old man said. "People might forget. You give us the idea, so we had them cut the words into the stone. We were hoping you meant it."

17

Dear Lucille,

Cheating on an exam? Are you kidding me? When I was in school, there was an honor code. We had to sign the cover of those blue exam books, "Pledge no aid, no violations." And sign our name. I mean, you'd think it wouldn't make a difference, but there was something about signing your name to a pledge. These days, I wonder what they do. Do the teachers talk about honesty at all? It's a lot of pressure on those kids. All about testing and scores. Thinking for yourself – what we used to call self-reliance? Who does that anymore? How is he going to learn to be his own man?

I'm glad Jack sat him down. If he had taken a belt to him, I wouldn't have been happy, but I would have understood. Brad has to be made to understand that if you start bending the truth, there's no telling where it will lead. You end up not being straight with anybody. How can you have any friends – close friends – if you don't know how to earn a person's trust?

On the force, there's not just trust but loyalty – another old-fashioned word. Most of us came out of the military, and no one needed to explain it. You don't get to make your own decisions about which orders to follow. That's where the truth comes in. You're never cutting corners. In a war, they tell you there are some people who need to be killed. I really can't talk about this. Don't know how I got started, but I'm going to send this anyway because I don't know how to make it clearer. It's easier to take drastic measures when the decision comes from above, especially when you don't know who actually made the decision and issued the order. You follow. There's a danger, of course. But how else would anything bad ever get done – when it's clear that going by the book won't get the problem solved?

I don't want to add to the pressure, but I do hope and expect that Bradley will go to college. I already sent you that money of Clara's, and I don't expect you to set it aside. There are things he'll need now, and I can't have you spending your own on him. It just wouldn't be fair. But thinking about the loyalty, I can tell you I've been on the force long enough to have some influential friends, friends who know how to get things done, how to make things right. Some breaks are coming my way. By the time Brad is ready for college I want the money to be there, and not by loading him or me up with loans it would take forever to pay off. As well, I want him and me to have a house where there are some trees and some clean air. I don't mean out in the country. I'm not about to retire. Somewhere near a junior college maybe.

Believe me, you have my support. Tell Jack I owe him for doing what's right.

Your loving brother,

Bert

18

On the first day of the hearing, Eli was seated with Keiko and Marcia Ellis at a counsel table on one side, and an attorney named Arnold Michelson sat with Oates and Torres on the other. In an inquest, counselors are not designated as plaintiff or defense, but they were seated as though they were. Facing them at a table in the center of the room was the hearing officer, who is not a judge because it's not a trial, but wields the same authority and calls all the shots. At an inquest, this role should be performed by the coroner, but instead of Sandoval, a severe-looking woman sat there. This was Judith Ferrara, his deputy, who would explain her being there in due course.

Nichols and Hughes sat by themselves, off to one side, near the referee's table and the stenographer.

Spectators were permitted, and Eli noticed familiar faces from the church – Evans, Dolores, Lionel, and Patrice, along with Reverend Jeffords. Bones took a seat with them in a row of chairs along the back.

Lawyers for the District Attorney's office were invited and did attend. But they sat out in the hall and not one of them ever ventured inside, for the duration of the inquest. They talked amongst themselves. Maybe they were baseball fans.

Eli thought jury selection had gone as expected, and the deck was already stacked against him. He used up his preemptory challenges on white males in ties. Michelson objected to anyone who looked to be working class and black. They ended up with nine men and five women – all white except for Evelyn, a mild-mannered Filipina, and Jonas, a distinguished-appearing African-American in a banker's suit and tie. Jonas was in the foreman's chair.

Once they were empaneled, Ferrara instructed the jury, "If you find the subject died at the hands of another person, that could be a matter for a criminal proceeding. But this is an inquest. Your job is simply to determine the cause of death, based on the medical evidence."

Eli piped up: "Your honor, I'd like to raise an objection."

She did not like him from the start and shot him an injured look. "Just what have I said?"

Eli asked her, "Why is the coroner not conducting this inquest himself?"

She sniffed and chose to direct her response to the jury box: "I am an attorney with the coroner's office, and I will be conducting this hearing on behalf of Coroner Sandoval. He will be testifying as an expert witness." Then she turned back to Eli with the hint of a sneer. "Anything further, Mr. Wolff?"

The plan was for Oates and Torres to take the witness stand to give their version of what happened that fateful evening.

It was Ferrara, then, who called Oates, who dutifully took his place at the front. He took his time and, Eli was surprised to see, was leaning heavily on a cane. No sooner was the officer seated than Michelson shot up. "Excuse me, Ms. Ferrara. Arnold Michelson. I represent Officers Oates and Torres. Under my instructions, the officers will assert the Fifth Amendment."

"Ms. Ferrara," Eli complained, "we understood that the officers might well assert those rights but that they would nevertheless stipulate to the facts of their attempt to arrest Mr. Ellis."

Ferrara said without a glance to Michelson, "There may be some disagreement about the facts or the interpretation of those facts, which the officers' representative here feels may be prejudicial to the interests of his clients. We do have the police report, as well as Coroner Sandoval's findings." She fingered the papers in front of her. "And such documents shall be entered into evidence at the appropriate time and summarized for the jury. I believe you gentlemen have copies and have had ample opportunity to read them?"

Both attorneys answered yes.

Ferrara turned to Michelson and said, "Your clients' assertion of their rights is noted." Then she asked Eli, "Questions, Mr. Wolff?"

Eli stood. "Mr. Oates, is it true you applied a carotid control choke hold on Hank Ellis's neck with your baton until he lost consciousness and died?"

Oates looked to Michelson, who quickly responded, "Don't answer."

Ferrara's expression made it clear she expected no better from Eli. Rebuking him every time he got out of line might be a waste of time. Instead, she asked him, "Mr. Wolff, do you have any questions the officer *can* answer?"

"Apparently not," Eli muttered, and he sat down.

"Thank you, officer," she said. "You are excused."

Then, Torres took the stand, and his expression was impassive.

Eli asked him, "Officer Torres, is it true that Hank Ellis had no weapon?"

"Don't answer that question," Michelson advised. "Same objection."

"Well, either it's a fact, or it isn't!" Eli exclaimed. "Is holding a weapon a matter of opinion?"

"It may be if the light is bad. This was dusk, don't forget," Michelson said. "Existence of a weapon goes to self-defense, and we're talking cause of death here, not provocation, am I right?"

"Are you gentlemen finished chatting?" Ferrara asked. When neither of them said anything, she again addressed the jury. "Counsel's questions are highly suggestive. You are not to construe them as evidence or consider them in reaching your verdict."

And, without having to say a word, Torres was done. It made Eli wonder why those cops were even in the room.

Sandoval hadn't been in attendance so far, but as Torres returned to his seat, the coroner came in the door as if summoned by some silent signal. On his gaunt frame hung an impeccably tailored dark-gray chalk-stripe suit. He wore a crisp white linen shirt with French cuffs and a muted paisley silk tie. If his teeth hadn't been yellow with tobacco stains, he could be a high-salary movie-star villain. But with that filthy smile, he could still be the president of some third-world country.

Eli had expected to go first in questioning new witnesses, but for no apparent reason, Ferrara prompted Michelson to begin.

"Doctor," Michelson said respectfully as he hoisted the document, "I am looking at your report. In layman's terms, is this man's heart problem something we all might have sooner or later?"

"Yes," Sandoval said. "But it's rare at such a young age. He was twenty-nine, I believe."

"But you did find heart disease?"

"Very definitely."

"And this condition would restrict blood flow?"

"Yes, decidedly."

"So," and here Michelson was hitting his stride, "if this person were involved in an altercation lasting several minutes, it would be difficult for him to maintain a normal blood flow?"

Sandoval turned toward the jury to explain, "With this kind of disease, the heart cannot increase its cardiac output during exertion. An arrhythmia could occur."

It seemed Michelson was stating a conclusion when he asked, "Such a person would be at risk much of the time, wouldn't he?" Eli wondered how it fell to this guy, as attorney for the cops, to serve as Sandoval's shill. Ferrara could have done as much, and probably should have. But as much as everyone was supposed to pretend this wasn't a trial and there would be no finding of specific fault, the jury – and especially the spectators – wanted this to be a trial. If, by some quirk, Eli were to prevail and the jury found that Hank had died "at the hands of another," the cops would be cooked. In the real world, they wouldn't be charged as criminals, but they might draw reprimands and lose their pensions. And, more important in the scheme of things, the department would be shamed.

To make sure the jury got the picture, Sandoval added, "He could have a cardiac arrest at any time – with minimal excitement – even during sleep."

So, they could have whispered to Hank, and it killed him?

Michelson summarized again, which was sure to be out of order, but Eli was beginning to realize he'd better save his outbursts for later: "Therefore, you cannot say with certainty, Doctor, whether this scuffle caused this man's death?"

Scuffle? More than a whisper? Was it less than, say, fisticuffs?

Eli was not about to make an issue of Hank's age. The jury might know that black men were prone to hardening of the arteries and high blood pressure – consequences of a high-fat diet of ribs, fried chicken, and greens cooked in lard. Aunt Kizzie's cuisine was not on trial here, but it might as well be – the implication being if you eat like that, you deserve to die.

Sandoval's eyes narrowed as he grew wistful. Was he straining to see the truth through a thick fog of hypocrisy? "There is some doubt in my mind," he mused. "If he had exerted himself just before the incident – jogging or emotional strain? Or sexual activity. Any of those stress factors could be the triggering mechanism."

So, it wasn't his diet that killed Hank but the sad fact that he must have been banging some hooker while his wife was away? Deserve to die? In that case, he deserved to burn.

Now it was Ferrara's turn to take her whack at the dead man. "Let me be clear about this," she said as she peered into the artificial fog. "The man's heart gave out, but not necessarily because of the altercation?"

Sandoval exuded scrupulous honesty when he declared, "Medically, there is no way to tell."

An uneasy muttering came from the crowd in the back. Eli could hear Evans' low growl but couldn't make out the words.

Michelson rose to say, "Thank you, Doctor." And then to Ferrara, "Nothing further."

"Counsel?" Ferrara indicated Eli could finally have at Sandoval.

Eli had a copy of a glossy magazine with Sandoval's portrait on the cover. He waved it at the jury as he approached the witness.

"Coroner Sandoval, are you aware that the press calls you Dr. Morbid?"

Ferrara huffed, "Relevance, Mr. Wolff?"

"I have a point, your honor, if you'll permit me?"

"Proceed," she said reluctantly.

Keeping his cool and no doubt flattered, Sandoval replied, "I study the medical effects of death. I don't cause it, despite what my overworked staff might tell you."

He didn't get a laugh, but Michelson smiled.

"But you excuse it?" Eli asked the coroner. "Justify it?"

"I don't follow," Dr. Morbid said.

"They also call you the Celebrity Coroner, I believe. Why is that?"

"When famous people die under mysterious circumstances, it's news. Some of those people are, let's say, self-destructive despite – or perhaps because of – their fame."

Some philosopher, this guy.

"You are routinely involved in examining cases of officer-involved shootings, are you not?"

"These things happen. Regrettably," Sandoval said.

Then Eli asked, "Doctor, has your department ever attributed the cause of a shooting death to, say, lead poisoning?"

This one drew laughter from the spectators, which got Ferrara fuming.

"Mr. Wolff," she said, "one more frivolous, pointless question and you will be subject to disciplinary action."

Sandoval remained composed and polite, not offended but bemused. "What you are suggesting would be unthinkable, ridiculous."

"Attributing a brutal beating death to the condition of the victim's arteries – isn't that just as ridiculous?" Eli stared at Ferrara. She didn't dare consider this a frivolous question.

The doctor decided to fall back on his official line and answered, "As I said, I can only speculate as to the triggering mechanism."

This got a grumble from Evans, which set off Ferrara.

"That's enough!" she shouted. "We'll have order!" She instructed Sandoval, "Don't answer that." She announced, "We'll take a fifteen-minute recess," and she glared at Eli as she ordered, "Counsel, I'll see you in chambers."

"CHAMBERS" was Sandoval's office, and Ferrara didn't mind at all sitting in his enormous leather chair. Eli sat and didn't slouch, ready to take whatever rebuke she felt he had coming.

In private, she wasn't nearly as angry as she should have been. "I've had enough of your antics. This isn't some cheap P-I case. And you're making us all look bad."

"Where's the D-A?" Eli wanted to know. "Bound and gagged in some closet?"

Perhaps it didn't deserve an answer. How the District Attorney managed his staff was not her concern. "Okay, maybe you're not some jerk-off ambulance chaser, but what does it get you annoying the hell out of me and teasing my witnesses?"

"Sorry," Eli said. "There's a murdered corpse in that room, and you are politely suggesting to the jury it doesn't stink."

"We both have a job to do here, whether it meets with your approval or not."

"The twisted logic of the coroner's report doesn't bother you even a little bit? You actually expect a jury to buy that story?"

"We have to deal with medical facts," she told him. "You go on about sixty blows to the body and choking? Those facts are not yet in evidence. Basic procedure, Mr. Wolff!"

"Sandoval knows goddamn well what he saw. Once he's off the stand, the jury wouldn't have the chance to see the look on his face when confronted with those facts."

"The jury does not at this point know what he saw. Bring on your expert witness. Let them hear it from her. Build a case and cut out all this name-calling." Then she added, "You know she used to work for him."

"I heard he wanted a closer working relationship."

"Well, for whatever reason, these days she's on the outside, and it's still his store. You learn in public service it's all about compromise. Or you don't get anything done. I expect Dr. Tamura is better off in private practice."

"Is that what I should tell Marcia Ellis? That this case is all about compromise? She's not just sucking for bucks here, you know. She wants her husband vindicated. She thinks he was a stand-up guy."

Ferrara gave him a look that said they were done.

"From now on," she said, "your questions had better be relevant. And courteous. Or you'll find yourself in jail for contempt."

"Throw me in jail and you might as well take out an ad that this show is rigged."

She might have wanted to say more, but all she could manage was, "Don't count on getting some kind of sensational result. You're out of your league. But you will be heard."

∼

ON HIS WAY out of his meeting with Ferrara, Eli saw Chief Nichols in the hallway talking to Oates and Torres. Nichols was dressed in a three-piece suit, and the two officers were in uniform. Oates was leaning on his cane. Eli went over to them.

He asked Nichols, "Did you know about Danny Ellis? Murdered."

"Under investigation," the Chief said. "As a rule, crack dealers don't live that long."

Indicating the cane, Eli said to Oates, "Going for the sympathy angle?"

"Piece of land mine I picked up when you were in diapers," Oates explained. "When it acts up, they put me on the desk."

Eli sniffed. "You might want to lighten up on the aftershave."

BACK IN THE HEARING ROOM, Sandoval was still on the witness stand. Eli was showing him some glossy photos.

"Doctor, referring to photograph number five, did you find a lateral contusion on the left side of the victim's neck?"

"Objection, your honor," shouted Michelson. "Victim?"

"Strike the word *victim* from the record," Ferrara instructed. "You know better than that, Mr. Wolff."

Eli nodded courteously and rephrased, "Was there a mark on the neck of the unfortunate deceased subject Hank Ellis?"

"He was wearing a T-shirt," Sandoval said and pointed to the photo. "This mark is consistent with someone pulling on the shirt, the margin of the neckline cutting into the skin."

In the back, Evans was grumbling again.

"That's the only possible explanation?" Eli asked.

"It's the most plausible, I think," Sandoval said.

"And referring to photo number eleven, did you find, just below that linear mark, three crescent-shaped, recent red-brown abrasions?"

Sandoval took the picture and studied it briefly.

"Yes, also noted in my report."

"Do you have an opinion as to what caused those marks?"

"Fingernails," the doctor replied.

"Is it possible those were Hank Ellis's own fingernail marks?"

"If we had taken fingernail clippings of the subject, we'd know," Sandoval said. "But I'm not sure that was done."

"Perhaps he was trying to move some object away from his neck? Relieve the pressure? Get air into his lungs? To fight off, I don't know, being choked to death?"

An angry buzz came from the back.

"Or," Sandoval said, nonplussed, "in the heat of passion that night, his partner tore at his T-shirt and scratched his neck."

Marcia Ellis winced, and Evans shouted, "That's an insult!"

Ferrara shouted back, "Another outburst, sir, and I will have the bailiff escort you from the room."

Eli came closer to Sandoval and said, "Sex is a big topic with you, isn't it?"

The laughter in the room relieved some of the tension.

"Counselor!" Ferrara scolded.

"Okay, okay. My apologies to the court. I get carried away." Eli said to her and then turned back to Sandoval. "Doctor, if someone has a heart attack, wouldn't you expect to find a blood clot, muscle damage to the heart, or both?"

"Yes," he said.

"But you didn't find either of these conditions in the heart of Hank Ellis, did you?"

"No, I did not."

"Then why are you so vehement he died of some kind of heart condition?"

"Because," Sandoval stated evenly, "that's what he had."

"Because – *why?*"

"Because it's the truth."

Eli was trying to remain respectful. "Doctor, did you find any evidence that might lead you to a possible hypothesis of death by asphyxiation?"

"No," Sandoval said flatly. "Nothing."

"Isn't the medical evidence also consistent with the possibility that Hank Ellis was choked to death?"

"Objection," said Michelson. "Basis."

Once again, Ferrara was tutoring Eli. "Mr. Wolff, you need a basis to speculate about asphyxiation. The coroner's report doesn't raise that possibility."

"I apologize, Ms. Ferrara," Eli said, "if once again it seems I have the procedure all wrong. It may seem I'm putting the cart before the horse. But in this case, we're in a situation where the good doctor tells us there is no horse. *No horse?* When there's horse manure all over the place? Go figure!"

Amazingly, Ferrara did not cite him then and there. "Facts not in evidence, Mr. Wolff. Perhaps I should make you stay after school and write it a thousand times. Build your case. Present the facts, then your hypotheses, if relevant."

"Do I get to recall Coroner Sandoval so he can stipulate to the existence of a horse were such then in evidence?"

Ferrara and the coroner exchanged cautious looks. Ferrara said, "If his schedule permits. The coroner has other responsibilities, you know."

Returning to Sandoval, Eli said, "All right, then. Respectfully. Let me put it to you this way. If Hank Ellis didn't have this fight with the police, do you think he would still be alive today?"

Sandoval was getting bored. "I can't be certain."

"Are you saying he might have died anyway? Suddenly? Then and there? Without the police?"

"I'm not necessarily saying that."

"Okay, then. What else could have happened to make him die at that particular moment?"

Sandoval took a deep breath. "As I have stated, and I thought I made myself clear. Any kind of stress. Physical. Emotional."

"From having sex, you mean?"

Sandoval rolled his eyes. Ferrara was about to speak, but Eli stopped her with "No further questions at this time."

Eli returned to his seat and gave Marcia a reassuring touch on the shoulder.

"Thank you, Doctor," Ferrara said. "You are excused." Sandoval stepped down and immediately left the room. Eli suspected they wouldn't be seeing him again.

It was late on Friday. Ferrara announced, "We are about to recess for the weekend. Mr. Wolff, can you tell us now what witnesses you will be calling when we reconvene?"

"Certainly," Eli said. "Dr. Keiko Tamura and Cynthia Holoman."

Ferrara frowned and pretended to study her notes. "Cynthia Holoman? I don't believe I have that name. Is she one of your experts?"

"She's an eyewitness, Ms. Ferrara."

Michelson shared a look with Oates and Torres.

Ferrara said, "We don't have depositions from any eyewitnesses but Daniel Ellis."

Eli asked, "Are you aware that Daniel Ellis is recently deceased?"

"Yes," she said. "What's your point?"

"Mr. Daniel Ellis, a material witness in this proceeding, was murdered a week ago Tuesday."

There was a murmur among the spectators, but this was not news to them, nor probably to anyone in the room.

"Counselor," she said, "regrettable as that might be, we have the man's sworn statement. Now, what else do you have?"

"Understandably, Ms. Holoman has been in fear for her life," Eli said. "But we have persuaded her to come forward."

"Perhaps she should be placed in protective custody," Ferrara suggested.

Eli came back with "By the *police?*"

This got a laugh, which annoyed Ferrara once again.

"We'll have order!" she shouted.

"If you have no objection, your honor," Eli said, "we'll take our chances on the outside."

Ferrara didn't ask but stated firmly, "Her safety will be your responsibility, then."

"Yes," Eli said.

"We'll stand in recess until nine A-M Monday."

~

OUTSIDE, Eli saw Chief Nichols about to get into his black stretch limousine as his driver held the rear door.

Eli strode up. "Nice ride! City vehicle? Is this in the motor pool or just a day rental?"

Nichols didn't bother to raise his voice to say, "They don't need to make you look silly in there. You're doing a good job of that yourself."

Nichols slid in, and the driver shut the door.

~

THAT NIGHT, Eli had more than the usual trouble falling asleep. He worried that he'd bring Marcia Ellis nothing but more grief. He was hoping for a settlement, but all they might get this time out would be a finding that would *sugges*t a crime. Then his team would need to have a long think about what to do next – and how to pay for it. It was difficult to imagine the DA would ever bring charges against those cops.

And as for closure for Marcia, Eli didn't believe in the term. *Closure,* in his mind, was a euphemism for *revenge.* Legal, sanctioned retribution. An eye for an eye. A life for a life.

He fretted that he'd done nothing so far to find Marco Gutierrez.

Why can't Vince help Gabe find his kid?

19

Dear Lucille,

There is only one way to stand up to a bully. We're not talking about the kind of person who listens to reason or who respects any kind of authority. Guys like that respect strength and they bow only to blunt force. I see it every day.

It's really simple. I'm sure Jack knows. When it's self-defense, the rules don't apply. It's wrong for them to come at you. It's wrong for them to hit you, whether it's provoked or unprovoked. (Guys get drunk, they ignore all the rules, but that's the way some are. Human nature won't change anytime soon.)

If you get hit, you hit back with everything you've got, with anything you can find. There's no decision to make when you're afraid for your life. Every living creature has the God-given right to do whatever is necessary to survive.

Tell Jack to tell him and I'll back him up any day. You don't run. You don't talk. You don't wait. You hit back harder than you got.

If he gets expelled for something like that, you can send him back to me, and I'll buy him the thickest steak in town.

Sorry, I'm letting off steam.

Your loving brother,

Bert

20

E li worked into the night on Friday, holed up in Bones' office. He used pushpins to tack up index cards on a corkboard. One side was labeled TACTICS, the other side EVIDENCE. The tactics list was much longer than the evidence. And there were a lot of cards with hasty scratchings-out strewn around him on the floor.

He'd just put a line through another lame idea on the tactics list when the phone rang. It was awfully late for anyone to be calling Bones, and his first thought was that Keiko might be in trouble.

"Wolff."

A kid's voice asked, "That you, *abogado?*"

"Ramon! You okay?"

"I see that guy again," he said.

"You stay away from him, you hear? Are you okay? What did he do?"

"Gimme another twenty, is all."

Eli's mind raced. "Where are you calling from? You're not with him now, are you? You got school tomorrow – does your mother know you're up? Ramon, please, please tell me you're okay."

"Me, I got no problem, but the *vato* says you do."

"Tell me he's not there with you!"

"I was in front of my house, they drive by. They gimme the cash, and they go."

"They? Tell me what they looked like! Was it a police car?"

"I gotta go, man. This guy says tell Eli he don't live through the weekend. Your girlfriend, too."

"Ramon, if these guys come back – run the other way and tell someone!"

"It's not a game, is it *abogado*? Be safe."

And the line went dead.

Eli's heart was pounding. It wasn't the first time he'd been threatened, and in some ways he'd expected it – especially since it was no secret where he was staying. And calling the police seemed pointless. But putting the kid in harm's way made it all the more chilling.

Surely they wouldn't dare hurt Ramon?

In a way, receiving a threat by whatever means was a hopeful sign. First of all, it meant someone was seriously afraid he'd win his case. And second, if they want you to be dead, they don't warn you first. No, they wanted him to withdraw from the case. Or simply get out of town, don't bother to show up on Monday, and lose by default. If he ran away, they'd need some story, and perhaps even some fabricated evidence, about how he'd gone missing – just so some newshound wouldn't get the idea they'd killed him and raise enough suspicion to trigger an investigation. Ferrara and the public would have to think he'd lost his nerve, and the cover story would blame black activists for chasing him off. He'd be replaced by some tame Oreo cookie who'd been paid off.

When the phone rang again, Eli snatched it up.

"Ramon, listen to me –"

But it wasn't Ramon. It was Keiko, and she was sobbing. "Eli? Somebody just threatened to kill me."

ELI HAD an idea where they could go for the weekend. Neither of them had any intention of skipping out on the hearing. They didn't share any details on the phone. He just told her he'd be picking her up as soon as he could get there. He threw some things in a suitcase he borrowed from Bones, who was supposed to be his protector at the house but just now was nowhere to be seen. Eli should have worried that his friend was out so late, but the likely explanation (absent the present circumstances) would be a hookup with a girlfriend – past, present, or future. As he locked up the place and threw his bag in the back of the Chevette, Eli decided he had enough to worry about.

By now it was two in the morning. A quick route to Keiko's would have been to take the expressway. And considering that the interstates were the jurisdiction of the state troopers and not local cops, it should have been a safer route. But tonight Eli had a cautious man's fear of risk from any direction. He surmised traffic would be light on the expressway, which would encourage speeders, and too many of them at this hour would be driving drunk after the bar closings.

He resolved to stick to surface streets, where traffic might also be light but erratic drivers easier to spot before they slammed into him. He'd take surface streets – all wide, well-lit boulevards where he could at least count on there being gapers as witnesses to any mishap, accidental or otherwise.

The cruise down the boulevard was uneventful, and traffic was sparse. He'd just passed a major intersection when he noticed a pair of headlights pulling up behind him and following closely. There was nothing to prevent them from pulling around, so when they stayed with him, he knew he was in trouble. He veered right abruptly at the next light. It was an instinctive fake-out until he realized his pursuers might not know he was deviating from his planned route. They took the turn with him, and both cars proceeded north.

Now they were tailgating him, practically touching.

Eli took the first opportunity to turn, now heading east. The pavement was rougher, with twists and turns as the road wended through the hills. No sooner had he made the turn than the other car bumped his rear fender, then bumped it again. Back on the boulevard, it would have been impossible for the little Chevette to outrun just about any chase car. But here as the road got curvy, it occurred to Eli that his edge might be maneuverability. He kicked the shift into low and floored it, careening momentarily away.

The other car betrayed its high-cube engine as it roared in anger and accelerated powerfully to close the gap. But the Chevette held the road tightly as the bigger car's tires squealed in protest as it dodged and weaved.

They were doing ninety-plus down this dark, empty surface street as they lurched and kicked over bumps, gravel, and ruts.

Eli was already bathed in the headlights when he was suddenly blinded by a series of dazzling flashes. They were harassing him with their high beams – *and leaning on the horn!* Eli responded by downshifting again, but his kiddie car was already maxed out.

Just as suddenly, there was a loud *screech,* and the glare dimmed fast. Unaccountably, the other car had slammed on its brakes and fallen back.

Eli tapped his brakes and slowed to nearer the speed limit so he wouldn't be tempting fate on the next hard curve. He was looking for a driveway or a side road – any turnout he could use, maybe go farther and douse his lights.

Then came the *roar* and the loud *squeal* again, like a great beast summoning all its strength for the death blow.

The other car closed rapidly and pulled into the passing lane beside him.

It was a low-rider '62 Impala – painted metallic orange, as irony would have it. There were six insanely drunk gang-bangers inside.

Their arms waved out the open windows. They cackled as they flipped him off, then the car sped out ahead, the tiny circles of its distinctive taillights disappearing into the distance.

Eli pulled the Chevette onto the shoulder, stopped, and switched off the ignition. He rolled down the window and sat there in the darkness for a long while as took in big gulps of air to get his heart rate under control.

No other cars passed by. The bangers didn't return, and the crickets told him the only thing to do when you're afraid is sing.

SOMEONE COULD HAVE HIRED *those gang-bangers.*

You could call it paranoia or self-fulfilling prophecy. Or maybe he'd made himself a target by driving so slowly.

He decided not to tell Keiko. She'd just agree with the crickets.

The Tamura house was a modest stucco bungalow on a cul-de-sac. At this hour, it was the only place on the street with a light on. There were crickets here, too. And tree frogs.

The interior was a mixture of Japanese and modernist American décor. Eli and Keiko sat on a low divan facing a Bonsai tree perched on a bent-plywood Eames coffee table. Keiko's packed overnight bag was at her feet. Eli had no desire to stay, but she explained that her grandmother insisted on serving them tea.

Eli was nervous. "We should have met somewhere. What if I was followed? And how can you leave her here? Shouldn't we be taking her with us?"

Keiko explained quietly, "She has advised me to go. She feels safest in her home, and she is used to fending for herself. However, she worries I may invite danger, and she certainly does not wish to be taken to it. I have also explained that after Monday – after I have had a chance to testify – it would be pointless for anyone to bring harm to me or my family. It is you and I who are vulnerable now, but only for a short time."

"I'd agree that whoever threatened us doesn't want us to see Monday," Eli sighed.

Fusako Tamura came in carrying a tea set on a silver tray. She was a prim and elegant woman in a plain housecoat. She set the tray in front of them and then sat down next to Eli on the divan.

Fusako looked at Keiko, who looked at Eli. It took him a moment to figure out he was supposed to make the next move.

"Would you do us the honor of pouring tea?" Keiko asked him.

Eli guessed correctly he should fill Fusako's cup first. After he poured Keiko's, he was going to do his own when she put out a hand to stop him. "Please allow her to pour for you."

Without a word, Fusako filled his cup, and they sat there sipping.

Then, Fusako set her cup down and looked up. Keiko said to Eli, "My grandmother has something for you."

"Oh, please, Mrs. Tamura," Eli said. "We can get breakfast on the road. We really should be going."

Keiko shook her head. He assumed Fusako had baked a traditional pastry to go with the tea.

Fusako got up and left the room. She returned in a moment carrying an ebony case about the size of a cigar box. Eli stood and bowed slightly as he'd seen some do as she held it out for him. He opened the lid to find a nickel-plated .38 caliber revolver. It wasn't new, but from the smell of machine oil, it had been recently cleaned.

"I'm sorry," he flushed. "I'm more of a you-can-negotiate-anything kind of guy."

"You take it," Fusako said firmly. As he took the box from her, she reached into the pocket of her housecoat and brought out a box of ammunition. Before she made a presentation of it, she added, "Always keep the bullets separate. Unless you are expecting company soon."

She lifted the gun out of the box and popped the cylinder open with an expert flick of the wrist.

"See? Empty," she said.

The timing of the doorbell ring was unfortunate. Eli held tight to the box of bullets, and Fusako still had the gun. No one thought to load it.

When the knocking came – in a hasty, rhythmic pattern as if meant to be code – Eli crossed to the door and looked out the peep-hole.

It was Bones, who must have switched off his car headlights and glided his Coupe de Ville to a quiet stop at the curb.

"Where have you been?" Eli asked as he let him in.

"Had to make a run all the way over to the next county. Bring a brother home."

He was not surprised to see an older woman in a housecoat holding a revolver. All he said was "Ma'am" and gave a wink to Keiko.

Turning back to Eli, he fumed, "I'm thinking of making cremations cash in advance. You think that's tacky? I have to out-source it, and if I don't pay up quick, maybe they don't take my business. The last thing I want is a backlog – know what I mean?"

"We got threats," Eli said.

"Yeah, Keiko left me a message, which is more than you had the sense to do." Handing Eli he keys, he said, "You take my car, and I'll drive the little red wagon. Best we switch."

They took the empty gun along with the box of bullets, and they said good-bye to Fusasko, who insisted she didn't want to know where they were going.

Outside, Eli said to Bones, "You're taking a risk as it is, but I'd feel better about this if you were coming."

"I gotta get this guy to his last barbeque, then I try and make good on your lying promises."

"Somebody's talking?"

"I got a line on Cyndi. I think I know where she's at, but getting her to talk's another thing. Not to mention keeping her breathing until Monday and making sure she shows up."

"Wow. We get her on the stand, we'll all be safer. What's the problem?"

"They say she wants fifty thousand."

"Don't make her any promises, or they won't believe anything she says. And it's just slightly illegal."

Before Eli got behind the wheel of the Cadillac, he gave Bones a hug. "Thanks, man."

"Back atcha," Bones said. "But you put one scratch on my car and our love affair will be a distant memory."

21

T he road to Eli's planned hiding place in the country is long and lonely, especially in the dark hours before dawn. On the expressway, after you get past the outer exurbs and the bejeweled carpet that is the sprawling city at night, the terrain is flat, uninspiring, and cavernously dark if there is no Moon. Your companions on the road are mostly semi-trailer trucks carrying foreign-made goods from the docks in the harbor to the superstores of the country's interior.

Eli and Keiko were headed, not for a glitzy resort, but to a little health spa tucked away in a rural area surrounded by scrub woodland and dusty backroads. Eli knew the owners, Vivek and Myra Singhe, who ran a budget-priced retreat where hippies would go to meditate and drunks could dry out. The adjacent small town had dozens of resort hotels built around pools of hot lithium-laden water that seeps up from volcanic bedrock. But, over the years, that wealth of natural healing substance had not assured the commercial success of the place as a tourist destination. Fed by the melt-water of snows in the mountains to the south as well as by waters underground, the classier resorts had been preferred getaways since the days when celebrities who were either temporarily unemployed or trying to hide from the press, the Mob, or a jealous husband. The waters there did not bubble up hot, for the most part, but oozed out to nurture artificially rolling expanses of grass where these eclipsed stars and snowbird sales executives, the kings of the Rust Belt, could spend the mornings of the hot days strolling around telling dirty jokes while looking for the golf balls they'd lost in the rough.

So, the resorts were too high-profile, even though hiding among bewildered golfers might be suitable protective cover. He thought this little spa was the perfect place to lay low. Cops and nurses went there to retire in the mobile-home parks, and working couples from the city could buy a modest ranch house there if moving to adjacent tax-friendlier states would put them too far from ailing parents or cherished grandchildren.

Eli couldn't say why he thought the spa was a safe place to go. Maybe it was just that Myra was the kind of person who could steady you in a crisis. She and Vivek were gradually renovating a dozen tumbledown bungalows, and each time he visited, there was a new coat of paint or a sink had been replaced. The pace of change, like their lives, was incremental, deliberate, and even meditative. The Singhes were working toward their goal, as detached from the world as they could be and still operate a commercial enterprise to sustain their family. But, for all Eli knew, when they finally had the place looking first-class (or close enough), and their kids were grown, they'd sell out and move across the highway to some glassed-in condo on the edge of a fairway.

The big Cadillac sailed smoothly on its hydraulic suspension. The ride was monotonous and almost too quiet. Eli's fund of adrenaline was nearly gone. To keep himself awake, he tried facial contortions – alternating between grimaces and smiles. Keiko, who had never been one for small talk, hadn't said anything since they'd passed through a patch of gated communities with newly manufactured homes, which she informed him was an enclave of wealthy Asians, mostly Chinese, with a huge Buddhist temple that drew people from all over. If she thought his facial expressions odd, she didn't remark on them. When she wasn't staring out the window, where there was almost nothing to see, she was methodically loading and unloading cartridges to and from the revolver in her lap.

"I'm sorry I got you into this," he said finally.

"No, you're not. And I'm not sorry I'm involved. I was the one who warned you. I tried to tell you how impossible it was, how dangerous. But you didn't listen, and we both know this is something that needs to be done."

"But did you think they'd threaten us? And, I mean, my car..."

"Did I worry it would happen? No. Did I think it was a possibility? Yes."

"We won't be needing that, you know," he said, referring to the gun.

"If someone wants to hurt us, it will be useless. That's not to say we shouldn't have it."

"Do you know how to use it?"

"Yes, when I was growing up, I murdered many of my father's beer cans on our camping trips. How about you?"

"I'm a Jewish lawyer. What do you think?"

"Then I bring something to the team after all." And for the first time in hours, she smiled.

"You're the whole show, sweetheart," Eli said. "We get you on the stand on Monday, and they won't be able to mop up their mess. There won't be any point in hurting us, and why would they take that chance? We'll be on an equal footing with them then, and it'll be all about the evidence and our arguments. And that's a game I know I – we – can win."

"Let me tell you something," she said. "Before you get too excited. This case is not going to trial, no matter what you think you can prove. One way or the other, it stops at the inquest. And this might be a front-page story in the neighborhood paper, and they'll be talking about it in every barbershop in the community, but we'll get a couple of inches on back pages of the major dailies. Best we can do is a settlement. For them, that stops short of an admission of guilt, but it gets your client something. And it gets the community something. It's a step, and it puts the fat men on notice. Maybe they back off, maybe they pay some attention. Because if they don't, the next time it will be harder for them to sweep it away."

So much for small talk. Does this woman have any hobbies? Wrong time to ask.

~

BEFORE HE'D PICKED up Keiko, Eli phoned Myra to book their stay. He'd visited a few times, but he'd never taken Keiko there. He requested two bungalows, and Myra said it was a slow time just now and they'd have the place to themselves. She'd been reading the papers and asked whether everything was okay. He almost told her but decided instead to just say he and his star witness needed some concentrated prep time aided by relaxing soaks in the baths. He was prepared to regret his decision to stay there. He feared he was exposing his friends to more risk than they realized. If he and Keiko had to leave in a hurry, it would be better to have stayed with strangers, who would have no further information to offer. The impulse might be childish, but Eli was comforted by the idea that his hosts were his willing protectors, even if the only support they could provide besides shelter was emotional.

From the looks of the ramshackle gate at the entry to the courtyard, the Mantra Mineral Resort couldn't offer any physical protection. The gate in the cinderblock perimeter wall was a door panel made of corrugated fiberglass, the kind they use for roofing. It had a hasp and spring lock, but Eli found it propped open with a brick. There was a note from Myra in an envelope taped to the door. The envelope wasn't even sealed. She apologized for not being awake at 4 a.m. to greet them properly, and she gave the numbers of the bungalows, along with the two keys. Security was almost nonexistent, except Myra urged him to make sure the gate was locked behind him after they got unloaded. Eli guessed the main threats in this neck of the woods would be kids looking for trouble, animals looking for food, and sneak thieves looking for cash, booze, or drugs.

Keiko pushed past him, grabbed the note and the keys, and headed straight for one of the bungalows. He noticed she had the gun. They hadn't made a rest stop on the way, and Eli guessed her bladder was aching, as his was, from all that ceremonial tea. But he held it in long enough to take her bag from the trunk and deliver it to her doorstep. Then he got his bag, locked up the car, made sure the gate was secure, and went to get his key from Keiko.

Her door wasn't locked, so he left his bag on the porch, tapped on the door, and let himself in.

She was still in the bathroom. "Could I get my key?" he called out. "I kind of need to use the facilities, too."

"Go right ahead," she said as she came out wiping her face with a washcloth, the gun still in her other hand. "But no key. You're already home."

"I just wanted to respect your privacy."

"Will you go ahead and pee already? I can't bear to see you suffer."

"I'll close the door," he said as he unzipped and went in.

Then, when he came out, he announced, "I washed my hands."

"You'd better get unpacked. I'm exhausted, and I hope I can sleep like a rock in this desert air."

"Are you sure you wouldn't rather be alone?"

"I could be worried that we'd get killed. Or hurt. Or kidnapped. I could worry that we will blow the case or that my career – if I ever decide to do anything else – could be ruined. Worrying that you'd rape me when I used to have to coax you is not high on my list of concerns."

"Do you think you somehow had to convince me?"

"Let's just say your mind was on other things a lot of the time."

"Are you saying you want to get it on – *now?* I mean, maybe not right this minute, but this trip?"

"You may be offended to hear that I haven't given it any thought. Would you please get into your pajamas or whatever it is you do so you're ready for lights out?"

"I'm offended you don't remember."

"People do change. Apparently, you haven't."

"Listen," he said, coming closer. "I didn't want this to be personal. Yes, we're hiding out, but we do have a lot of prep to do for Monday, and I've had some thoughts I need to share. The last thing I want is for you to think I brought you here to put the moves on you."

"And, as I said, that's the last thing I'd worry about." Then she added, "Remember, I'm the one who dumped you."

"Are you kidding me?"

"I shouldn't have brought that up," she said and took her toiletry kit into the bathroom and closed the door.

THEY BOTH SLEPT SOUNDLY. They were simply too exhausted to be worried. The bed was narrow, a standard double, and it sagged in the middle. By turns, they slept in each other's arms, even though neither had reached out for an embrace. As Eli drifted off to sleep, he remembered the smell of her hair and the soap she used. And he realized that both the sharp intelligence he needed to win this case and the real source of his emotional comfort were here, just inches away.

She *dropped* me? *How do you figure? Either way, I was a fool.*

ELI WOKE BEFORE SHE DID. He pulled on a pair of jeans and a T-shirt, let himself quietly out, and soon found the urn of hot coffee Myra had set up with the breakfast things by the lithium pool, where a kind of greenhouse enclosed the steaming water. She had two big plastic containers of granola – one maple-flavored and the other plain – a vat of yogurt, and a small selection of oranges, red grapes, and bananas. People didn't come here for the food. And, from the looks of things, a low-priced getaway was the main attraction. He poured himself a Styrofoam cup, black, and walked over to the office, where he found Myra going over the accounts.

"Hey, where's Vivek?" he grinned as she rose to give him a hug.

"Gone to the hardware store for PVC pipe. Again. We should just order a truckload of it and store it in the back. The copper crap they put in this place is all Chinese, thinner than code, and it cracks and splits when you so much as look at it. Water leaks can be expensive, let me tell you. The PVC isn't to code, but then what's changed and who's counting? It does the job. Vivek has learned to do the repairs himself, and we don't have to raise our rates. Good to see you, by the way." She held out the city paper and the *Wall Street Journal*. "Newspaper?"

"The only papers that pay us any attention are sold in the 'hood. I suppose you don't get them out here."

"Obviously not. Amazing we get anything."

"But the *Journal?*"

"Vivek reads it. He's intense about following the stock market. We don't have any stocks, mind you. But he's into that like some men are into fantasy baseball. He frets about all those trades he could have made." And she laughed. "Do sit down and tell me the story of your life so far." Then, she leaned in and asked softly, "And pray why didn't you take the two cabins?"

"We're safer together," he said as he sat down and gulped the coffee.

"Oh, is it safety?"

Eli realized he'd slipped. She wasn't supposed to know.

"I have this irrational fear of rattlesnakes in the bed."

"We don't have those," she said with a straight face. "There are copperheads, but most of those creatures are very shy. I'm sure they are all over, but I haven't seen one in years. Somehow the only snakes we've had in the rooms are the nonpoisonous black ones. Looking for mice. On the few occasions, we've been happy to have them."

A snake in the room, whatever its stripe, would be a shocker. Are they pets in India?

"Thank you for having us."

"No trouble. As you can see, the place is empty. Is Monday, as they say, the big day for you?"

"Keiko – you'll meet her later – is my expert witness. Her specialty is forensic medicine, and we had her do an independent autopsy. Once I put her on the stand, there's no going back. We'll prove the cops murdered an innocent, unarmed man because they panicked when they couldn't control him."

"But even if you win, what does that achieve? I mean no disrespect."

"For the client and for me? Money. For the community, maybe some respect, maybe the hope that things might get better someday." He shrugged. "And all the publicity can't hurt my practice. Maybe I'll finally get some clients who take their advice and pay their bills. Speaking of which, I forgot to ask you about the room rate."

"There will be no charge," she said in all seriousness. "If it were up to me, it would help with our own expenses, naturally. But the season is almost upon us, no matter. And if Vivek found the charge, he'd tear it up."

Eli refilled his cup on his way back to the bungalow. He thought about pouring one for Keiko, but he couldn't remember what she took in it. Myra had hot water there and an assortment of exotic teas, so he'd be sure to mention it. For security reasons, he could hope that the Singhes had a dog to be a fierce protector of the property. Instead, there was a clutter of cats, probably most of them strays, for which bowls of dry-food pellets had been set out all over the place. A fat, fluffy gray one with yellow eyes and matted fur stared at him with disdain, as if he were the stray.

Keiko was not only dressed and with her face on but also enjoying a ceramic cupful of green tea. She'd brought her own supplies, including a heating coil. She wore a flowered top and shorts, and her bare legs were as lithe and stunning as ever.

"Did you sleep well?" she asked.

"I'd forgotten what it was like being next to you."

"It's remarkable what we can make ourselves forget, when we have a reason."

"There's not much out there. Dry cereal and fruit. Soymilk or almond. They're vegan."

"I'll look at the fruit. Let's not go out."

"Okay, let's not. Look, if this was a bad idea, I'll drive you back. Put you in a nice hotel downtown? I mean, who would know?"

"Whoever is following us, that's who," she said.

"What makes you so sure we're being followed? Look at this place. They'd have a hard time sneaking up on us."

"Let's assume they're never far away. Just because no one comes kicking in the door doesn't mean they don't know where we are."

"What do we do after you have your banana?"

"We go over your brief and make sure we cover all those points in my testimony. And you said you had some new thoughts."

"Well, the main thought I had was wondering why you think you were the one to dump me."

"I'm not ready to talk about that yet. And if you're not kidding about the banana, I'd like one. If it's not too bruised."

THEY HAD a hot soak in the bathhouse, followed by some splashing around in the chilly chlorinated swimming pool. By then, they were ready to work. They spread out their files and notepads on a picnic table under a big umbrella. Myra came by and offered to bring them a chilled bottle of wine, but they opted for lemonade, and she brought it along with a plate of BLT sandwiches made with tempeh instead of bacon. They ate happily, all business. In the heat of the afternoon, Keiko excused herself for a nap in the bungalow, and Eli had a snooze outside in a lawn chair. By all appearances, they were a couple of schoolteachers on a working vacation. Eli could tell Myra approved of Keiko, not that it mattered. Which, of course, it did.

The day had been uneventful, and they decided they'd venture out for dinner. By that time, Vivek had finished his chores, and he advised there were just four choices in town – a red-sauce Italian, two not-unauthentic Mexican, and one indifferent and mainly carryout Chinese. When Keiko protested she needed vegetables, they decided on the Chinese, and the place was only two blocks away. It was full of Hispanic working-class locals who'd brought their kids for a family night out. The noise level was almost unbearable, but the food wasn't all that bad.

Eli's fortune-cookie message said he'd have a hard time with a dark-haired woman. The ambiguity was intriguing.

By the time they made it back to the bungalow and locked the door behind them, they thought perhaps their paranoia was unfounded. Oates and Torres didn't dare. They were too much in the spotlight. But someone, probably someone close to the officers in the cop fraternity, had threatened them. Maybe it was an intimidation ploy to throw them off their game and gain some psychological advantage for Monday. Nothing that might not go on in professional sports or a mean-spirited political campaign.

Not long after the sun went down, the phone by the bed in the bungalow rang. Eli answered it, thinking it was Myra asking for last requests before she left the office for the evening. Instead, there was a brief pause, then the recording playback:

"Remember, I'm the one who dumped you."

"Are you kidding me?"

"I shouldn't have brought that up."

Eli slammed the phone down, then he ripped the cord out of the wall.

"Was that another threat?" Keiko asked.

"No," he said fuming. "Just playback of a recording. They're getting everything we say. Here."

They looked at each other like two people who had just been told they'd ingested fast-acting poison or received fatal doses of radiation.

"What can we do?" he asked pointlessly. "The tap might not be on the phone. I don't know how they do it, but it could be they have our case strategy – everything we said to each other out there."

Keiko didn't answer. She just got up and took the gun from where she'd set it on the dresser. She opened the revolver, spun the cylinder, snapped it back, and set it carefully on the nightstand on her side of the bed.

"Maybe we should leave. Now," he said. "I could take you back home, or back to be with Bones, or we could, I don't know, drive around all night."

"They obviously have no trouble following us. I don't see any point in leaving. The good news," she said calmly, "is that if they have all that, there may be no need to harm us."

They stayed in their clothes, and neither one of them slept that night.

They sat in silence for a long while. She was propped up in the bed, he in the armchair. There was no TV and not even a radio, imposed advantages of this getaway retreat that emphasized hot water, meditation, and sleep.

Eli finally said, "I thought all Japanese were little guys."

He'd forgotten to bring swim trunks, and miraculously she'd produced a pair from her bag, claiming they'd belonged to her father.

First the tea and then the trunks. Does she miss anything?

"My father was Hawaiian on his mother's side. A big fellow, actually."

"Where did he learn to shoot?"

"U.S. Army."

"I'm sorry I got you into this."

"I told you," she said. "I don't regret my decision. And it was I who warned you. Most strenuously."

"They're going to try to make you look foolish on the witness stand. Do you really think we're out of danger if they're sure they can do that?"

"I thought you were the razor-sharp legal mind. Those hacks on the city payroll should be no match for you."

"I deserve that. Cocky, that's me. And maybe that's why we're in this mess. But I'm beginning to get just what it is I do. Respect for the law makes a community possible. Without the law, it's all just, I don't know, gang warfare."

"Does this mean you're a man with a conscience now?"

"I was a pragmatist before, and nothing's changed. But maybe I have some perspective."

"Bones said you told the people in church your grandfather was in a concentration camp."

"He didn't like to talk about it, and I don't remember all that much. Does he think I made it all up? To score with the church crowd?"

"You could have. A pragmatist would have."

"Yeah, okay, I might exaggerate about some things, for effect. But it's the truth."

"What does being Jewish mean to you?"

This was not a discussion they'd had before. He wondered where she was going with this. "I don't know," he said.

"You see, that's a problem."

"That I'm not hung up on my family background? What possible difference could it make? We got pretty serious, didn't we? Or was I mistaken about that, too?"

"To be Jewish, a child's mother has to be Jewish. Right?"

"That's Jewish law, but what makes you think I care?"

"You have a right to be proud of your heritage. It may matter very much to you someday."

He thought she might be teasing him, and he chuckled. "Are you telling me you broke up with me because you're not Jewish?"

"That's exactly what I'm telling you."

"That's crazy! This is America, the world's melting pot. We're all mutts, and proud of it."

"People say they don't care about these things, but they do. They say there are no more race issues, but there are. My grandmother is very traditional."

"Your grandmother? This is about your *grandmother?*"

She looked away, and he realized she was sobbing quietly.

He crossed the room to sit next to her. He reached for her chin and turned her face up to him.

"It's silly," she sniffed. "People here can't read an Asian face. Inscrutable, they say. That's the stereotype, but it's the way things are. As if we have no feelings. I loved you, and yet some part of me resented you. Some things you will never share. And yet, my father the Hawaiian and my mother the Japanese? I saw them both the same, exotic and not white, but how did they see each other? As different as you and me, I think. Should we be honest about those things? Or just fuck and drink and eat, and forget who we really are?"

He kissed her. She didn't pull away, but she didn't lean into it, either. The moment came and went.

"These people don't need to kill you," he said softly. "If they can take every private moment away, if they can make you feel raped and violated, if they can make you afraid every waking moment of your life – the power is all theirs."

They left the light on and lay down. He held her through the night, and this time not because the mattress wouldn't support them.

22

They set out for downtown at five the next morning and drove straight to the courthouse. Eli had packed his suit, and Keiko complained she'd forgotten to bring heels, but he thought she looked lovely and professional. He couldn't imagine the jury, especially the men, even thinking she was capable of a lie. And there was the stereotype, perhaps working in their favor this time, of the smart Asian girl whose arm always shot up first in class.

Everybody knows that girl has all the answers.

Eli left the cash from his wallet on the nightstand for Myra along with a note apologizing for the damage to the phone. He didn't explain why he'd done it.

Keiko caught up on her sleep by dozing the whole way in the car. He resolved he'd have to catch a nap later in the afternoon. Once or twice he thought a van might be following them, but it was never the same one for very long.

Despite their arriving early, she wasn't on the witness stand until 9:30. Ferrara was presiding. Eli stood beside Marcia

Ellis at the counsel's table as he questioned Keiko. Arnold Michelson sat opposite them. Sandoval was nowhere to be seen, and neither were Oates or Torres. The now-familiar contingent from the church was there in the visitors' section, including Evans and Reverend Jeffords.

The jury looked downright sleepy. Eli raised his voice, hoping to command their attention, at least for the next few minutes: "Dr. Tamura, please define for us exactly what the coroner's report means by 'multiple contusions.'"

"There were more than sixty bruises on the man's body," she said, "consistent with the use of a police baton."

They'd agreed that, in most of her answers, she'd refer to Hank as "the man." Doing so would reinforce the impression that she was scientific and objective. The jury should not assume she knew this guy or his family or that she was moved to tears as she saw what a merciless beating had done to his powerful body.

"Now, would you please describe what you found in the neck area?" Eli asked. "Demonstrate, if you would, on what is affectionately known as Purvis over there." Eli didn't know why the medical techs gave the dummy that name. Given the gallows humor of the forensic lab, he assumed it was a colorful story. This one had the skin on half of its body peeled back so the musculature was exposed.

People are meat machines.

Keiko walked over to the dummy and used her pen to point to the long muscles in its neck. "The sterno-mastoid muscle – here – makes it possible for you to turn your head. Now, my neck is fairly small, and so is this dummy's. But on this man the muscle was quite thick and heavy. And I saw it was very badly bruised."

Eli wasn't sure how technical he should seem. "It was a linear type of bruise, was it not?" It was easy to get into the jargon, and he worried the jury would see him as a guy who'd done just enough homework to know a few answers to a quiz, which would have been a fair description of his performance in school.

"Yes," she answered. "About twenty centimeters long."

"Dr. Sandoval says the bruise was caused by violent pulling of Hank's T-shirt. Do you agree?"

"The mark on the surface of the skin is not deep, perhaps consistent with pulling the shirt. But beneath the skin, the hemorrhaging was severe, as if from forceful and sustained compression."

It's frustrating to argue the obvious. What could have made that long bruise but a baton?

But he had to take it step by step, closing off any basis for refutation or doubt. "Could that kind of compression be produced by, say, a man's thumb?"

"Unlikely to do that kind of damage, I think." She spread her hand across the dummy's neck. "And you'd find the other finger marks besides the thumb. There were none."

Okay, let's have her say it.

"What type of instrument, in your expert opinion, caused the mark on the skin and the bruise on the muscle beneath?"

Keiko looked straight at Ferrara when she said, "It's consistent with a baton. Held in place with considerable force for at least several minutes."

The visitors stirred, and Ferrara gaveled for quiet.

Eli picked up a police baton from the table and walked over to hand it to Keiko. "Would you demonstrate to the jury how that must have been done?"

She walked over to the dummy and stood to its right side and in back. "The person would have to be positioned about here." She encircled the dummy's neck with her arms, with one hand on each end of the baton. Then she pulled back to show how the choke hold would be applied on the diagonal. "The baton would have to be held against the neck something like this. After several minutes, asphyxiation and cardiac arrest would result."

Eli worried his next question would draw an objection, but he had to ask, "Why would a person do such a thing?"

And Michelson jumped up right on cue. "Objection. This witness has no particular expertise in either psychology or police procedure."

"Okay, then," Eli rephrased it, "why would such an injury be plausible under the circumstances?"

"He was a big man," she said. "It could have been difficult to subdue him with just body blows."

"Thank you, doctor," Eli said and indicated for her to resume her seat on the stand. When she had, he said, "Dr. Sandoval also testified to some crescent-shaped marks on the neck. Did you note those as well?"

"Fingernails," she said decisively. "I think it is reasonable to assume that if someone is trying to strangle you —"

Ferrara didn't even wait for Michelson to object and ordered the court reporter, "Strike that."

"Dr. Tamura," Eli continued, "do you agree with the coroner's findings regarding cardiac arrest?"

"No," Keiko said. "I do not."

"Why?"

"In autopsies, we see hardening of the arteries in the majority of adults. We mention it as being present, but we rarely give it as a cause of death unless we also find a blood clot." And she stared down Ferrara as she added, "Which wasn't there."

Well, if you're going to break the rules, you'd better hit with all you've got.

Eli asked Keiko, "Would your findings lead you to conclude that Hank Ellis died at the hands of someone else?"

Ferrara snapped at the reporter, "Strike the question." Then, to Eli, "That's for the jury to decide, Mr. Wolff."

"Thank you, doctor," Eli said pointedly to Keiko. "No further questions at this time." And he sat down. Marcia gave him a weak smile as if looking for reassurance he thought he'd scored. He gave her a big smile back, but he wasn't at all sure.

Michelson stood and said, "I have questions for this witness, your honor."

"Proceed, Mr. Michelson," Ferrara said.

Michelson strode out from behind his table, taking mid-court advantage – and center-stage in front of the jury – as he faced Keiko. "Dr. Tamura, you stated under direct examination that you were employed as a deputy medical examiner of this county for two years?"

How is that a question?

"That's right," she said.

"And during that time, what types of autopsies did you have occasion to perform?"

"Mostly auto accidents and drug overdoses."

"How many beating deaths?"

She had to think. "Including domestic battery cases? I don't know. About twenty."

"Twenty. In two years."

Also not a question.

"It's difficult to classify" was all she could say.

Michelson went on, almost as if this were some congenial job interview, "Do you perform autopsies in your current job?"

"No," Keiko said. "It's general practice. And some lab work."

"Dr. Tamura," Michelson said and tried not to smile, "besides your work on this case, when was the last time you actually performed a clinical autopsy?"

She hesitated just long enough for the jury to catch her embarrassment. "Three years ago."

Now, he bore down. He came close and leaned in on the edge of the stand. "Let me ask you this. Aside from what you believe you saw in this case, have you ever even seen, first-hand, a body on which the carotid choke hold was used?"

"Well, no," she said, barely audible.

"I'm sorry," Michelson boomed. "Would you please repeat your answer?"

"No," Keiko said firmly. "I have not."

Michelson shot a proud look to Ferrara as he said, "Thank you, doctor. You're excused."

Cooked and flayed. And I didn't like the way he said doctor.

WHEN ELI and Keiko were comparing notes in the courthouse hallway, Bones walked up to them with a skittish Cyndi Holloman on his arm. Bones took Eli aside as Cyndi ignored Keiko and rummaged in her purse.

"I had to drag her here," Bones said in a low voice. "I'm not so sure this is going to work."

Bones led him over to the girl.

Eli offered his hand and said, "Cyndi, I'm –"

"I know who you are," she said.

"Did you see it? Did you actually see them beating him?"

She averted her eyes. Bones took her arm. "You got to do right by Hank," he said. "For Danny, too."

"Danny knew," Eli insisted. "And he was protecting you."

"Look what it got him," she said.

Eli took her other arm. "That's why you have to tell everything you know. Once it's out in the open, they can't hurt you. The best way to protect yourself – to protect all of us – is to tell everybody what they did. Otherwise, they're going to keep saying it didn't happen."

"Fine words," she said. "But I got bills to pay. I got my kids to take care of."

"Don't you see? We're afraid you won't be safe unless you talk. It's not about money."

"What's it about then?"

"They raped you."

"Excuse me?" She cringed. "Who are you talking about? I didn't say nothing like that."

"That night, when they broke into Hank's, they violated him. And Danny. And you. It's an ugly feeling. It never goes away. Maybe you know what I mean?"

"Yes," she said. "I do."

"You want to feel better, you tell everybody in a loud, clear voice what they did to Hank."

"Maybe we got some pride left," Bones said to her as he started to lead her away.

"Think about it. Please," Eli said. He saw her whisper to him as they walked, and Bones turned back with a reassuring nod.

CYNDI TOOK THE STAND. Bones sat alongside Marcia and Eli. Oates and Torres, both in freshly starched uniforms, were there, sitting with Michelson. Eli noticed Oates had his cane propped against the chair. Nichols was in the back with Hughes and an aide, near the door, as if they all might need to slip out. Sandoval sat behind Ferrara.

Eli asked her, "Ms. Holloman, did you see the police enter Hank's apartment that night?"

"Yes."

"And where were you?"

Marcia and Cyndi exchanged looks. Marcia wasn't supposed to know that Hank and Danny had had girls over that night. Marcia could guess Danny brought the party, and she knew her husband didn't go chasing anything. But now he was dead, and so was Danny. She'd never know for sure. And who would trust anything this tramp said?

Cyndi explained, "When they came in, I'm on the couch. Danny run out of there, me with him."

"How could you see what happened?"

"Danny run off. I thought maybe he was going to get help, but who would that be? I didn't know what to do. I just froze, stayed just outside. Where I could see in. I mean, I just figured they were going to take him away was all. Then I'd let someone know. I didn't expect it, maybe they didn't either. I didn't figure Hank would fight back, and surely not what they went and did."

"What did they do? And please keep it to exactly what you saw and heard."

"The big guy –"

"Do you see him here in the room?"

She pointed him out, and Eli said, "You've indicated Officer Oates."

"The big guy bust in the bathroom door, and he pulls Hank out of there. Then he and the other guy –"

"Again," Eli said, "please point him out, if you can." And she did. "The witness has identified Officer Torres. Please continue."

"Those two are hitting him with their clubs, but they can't bring him down. He stumbles around like some big bear. He yells out, 'Get off me! What have I done?' That's when Mr. Oates slams Hank in the chest, knocks the air out of him. Then the other guy grabs him by the neck like he's trying to strangle Hank, but he's only using one hand. The other guy says, 'That won't work,' and he whacks Hank in the belly with that club. Hank bends over, and he spits out blood. Then the guy gets behind him, and he puts the club on Hank's neck and just pulls back hard. Mr. Torres yells, 'Bert, stop!' but he keeps doing it and yells back, 'You got a better idea?' Not much longer and Hank just goes down heavy onto the floor, like a knockout. He's lying with his face on the floor, and Mr. Oates starts kicking him, I guess to make sure he won't get back up. Mr. Torres is trying to put the cuffs on Hank, and Mr. Oates tells him to watch his sidearm. And Hank's got some life in him still because he groans and fidgets, and they still can't cuff him. That's when Mr. Oates does the thing with the club on his neck again, and he pulls back real hard. Mr. Torres tells him to stop again, but he won't. Then Hank doesn't move. He's not moving at all. Mr. Oates gets up and tells Mr. Torres, 'Better have him cuffed when they show up.'"

"Thank you, Ms. Holloman. We appreciate all the detail you can remember." Eli paused, then said, "Did you see Officer Norbert Oates choke Hank Ellis to death?"

Ferrara was right on it, saying, "Strike that!" to the reporter. "Counsel," she scowled at Eli, "you're way beyond the scope of this inquest with that one." And she told the jury, "I will remind you that you must not be concerned with what person or persons might have been at fault. And this witness had no way of knowing whether death had occurred at that point."

Eli's eyes scanned each one of them in the jury box, and he added, "I think we all know what happened. No further questions of this witness." And he sat down beside Marcia.

"I have a few, your honor," Michelson said.

"Proceed, counselor," Ferrara said.

Michelson stood but stayed behind the table. "Ms. Holoman, what is your profession?"

"Why, I'm a dancer."

"What kind of dancer?"

Eli spoke up, "Objection. Relevance?"

Ferrara said, "Goes to credibility. The witness will answer."

"Exotic dancer," Cyndi said quietly.

Some on the jury, including Jonas, mumbled their disapproval.

"Ms. Holloman," Michelson went on, "isn't it true you earn your living as a prostitute?"

"Don't answer that!" Eli yelled.

Ferrara shot back, "Fifth Amendment, Mr. Wolff?"

"Why not," Eli replied. "It works for everybody else."

Then Ferrara asked Cyndi, "Were you induced in any way to testify today?"

"Induced?" Cyndi asked.

"Did counsel or anyone else promise you anything if you came and told us this story?"

"I asked for fifty thousand dollars, but they tell me that's not going to happen."

"Who told you? Mr. Wolff?" Ferrara asked, eager to have the answer.

"No," Cyndi said. "I never mentioned it to him. I asked Mr. Jackson, and he told me witnesses don't get money. Unless you're some doctor or scientist, then they might pay you a lot. I need money, too. I'm taking time out. I got kids. But I guess nobody cares."

Ferrara asked Eli, "Who is this Mr. Jackson?"

"That would be Luther Jackson," he replied, indicating his friend. "Proprietor of the funeral home that handled arrangements for Mrs. Ellis and also permitted Dr. Tamura to conduct her independent autopsy."

Ferrara asked Cyndi, "If no one offered you money, why are you here?"

Cyndi said simply, "Mr. Wolff told me if I told the truth, everybody would be safer."

"Safer?" Ferrara asked.

"One material witness has died," Eli explained. "Daniel Ellis, Ms. Holloman's boyfriend."

"I was given to understand, Mr. Wolff, that this Mr. Ellis was involved in criminal activity unrelated to this inquiry, activity which the police believe resulted in his death."

"That is the theory, Ms. Ferrara," Eli said. "Mr. Ellis was no choirboy. We're not asking this inquiry to make any connection, just to credit Ms. Holloman's version of events. Both she and Danny were there, and she's testifying today under oath, without inducement. And I might add, attempts by

Mr. Michelson here to impugn her reputation are unfair and prejudicial to the interests of my client and the truth being sought by these proceedings."

Ferrara had heard enough. Regarding both Michelson and Eli, she asked, "Are there no further questions of this witness?"

Michelson said, "Nothing further."

Ferrara seemed disappointed when Eli asked, "Would you permit me a few more?"

"You'd better be on point," she warned.

"Thank you," Eli said, and he approached the witness stand. "Cyndi, I apologize if anyone has insulted you here today. That was not my intention, and I want to thank you on behalf of all of us here for your cooperation and your willingness to speak the truth in spite of any pressure you might feel to keep quiet."

"Mr. Wolff, editorializing will not help your cause," Ferrara said. "Please get to it."

"Now, Cyndi. Think back to earlier that evening. After the police arrived. Where were you standing as the squad car pulled into the complex?"

"Theresa and me, we were down there with Hank. He's talking to them kids."

"What kids?"

"Setting off those firecrackers. Hank's telling them they could hurt themselves."

"And before you went upstairs, right before you went into

Hank's apartment, did you overhear a conversation between the officers?"

"Hearsay," Ferrara interjected. "Not admissible."

Eli asked her, "May I approach, your honor?"

She nodded, and he came up to say confidentially, "It's admissible if it establishes intent to commit a crime."

Her eyes grew large. She understood that not only was this the one exception to the hearsay rule but also it would be a kill shot at the cops. She glanced back to Sandoval, who shrugged, then over to Nichols, who thrust out his jaw. She knew neither one of them could object, but she had to check.

She wasn't ready to agree right away. "What's the substance of it?"

"They intended to beat him before they ever went in there," Eli said.

She hesitated. "I'll take it under advisement. Be prepared to recall her."

"Ms. Ferrara, I thought this would be an impartial inquest."

"Excuse me, counselor. Are you implying there's some type of collusion here?"

"I don't know about collusion, but there's certainly communication. You just checked in with two of them to see whether to let me do what we all know I have every right to do."

"I warned you about contempt."

Let's bet it all on red.

"Can you feel it?" Eli whispered in mock panic. "Which way the wind is blowing? You cite me for contempt and disallow this, there's going to be a firestorm in here!"

He couldn't have timed it better because just then she caught Evans' stare from the gallery, and the man looked like he was ready to strangle someone himself to even the score.

She announced loudly, "Repeat the question. The witness may answer."

Eli turned back to Cyndi. "What did you hear the officers say as they climbed the stairs to the balcony outside Hank's place?"

"The big one, he says to the other one —"

"Do you mean it was Officer Oates you heard?"

"Yes, I did." And she almost choked on the words, "He says, 'I think they could use some harassment.'"

"Come on, Cyndi. In a loud, clear voice."

"'I think they could use some harassment.' I heard it as good as I hear you now."

Eli glanced over to Nichols, who was speaking sotto but intently to Hughes. And then, sure enough, the top cop left the room.

"Thank you, Cyndi," Eli said. "Nothing further."

Ferrara cleared her throat and announced to the jury, "This reported conversation is a permitted exception to the hearsay rule. But it is of possibly dubious value and relevance. I would caution you strongly against putting any undue weight on this evidence in your deliberations. Again, your charge is to determine whether death was from natural causes or at the hands of another. If by another – whether there was intent to harm or it was an accident – could have a bearing on a criminal matter, but it should not affect your determination here. Mr. Wolff, I believe you have no other witnesses?"

"That's right. We have no more witnesses."

Sandoval came over and spoke briefly in Ferrara's ear. Then he left the room.

Ferrara said as she banged the gavel. "Staff has an administrative meeting tomorrow morning. We stand adjourned until two o'clock tomorrow afternoon."

Bug that meeting, and we'd learn a lot.

Eli thought he'd done a good job of turning up the heat, but then Marcia said to him, "It doesn't look so good for our side, does it? Everybody knows that Cyndi is a tramp."

Bones piped up, "Are you kidding? We're looking good today."

"It's like baseball or any of those games," she sighed. "No mud on your uniform? What does that get you?"

It made him wonder whether the visitors – and the jury – were thinking the same thing.

On the way out, he asked Bones, "Did you drive Cyndi over here?"

"Yeah, in your piece of shit Chevette, no disrespect to Generous Motors. She's waiting for me to take her back."

"Don't. Give her cab fare and don't let anybody see you do it. Or they'll say it was a wad of hundreds. Give her my card, and if she needs help, have her call me. Best stay out of it from now on."

He grinned. "I don't get to come back to see you lose?"

"I mean, stay the hell away from her. And, yes, I want you here when we nail those guys. Do we have a real bet this time?"

"I'm not about to jinx your case for your measly cash and a few crappy ego points."

23

That evening, Eli drove Keiko to her grandmother's and left her there, confident that she would now have no reason to use her weapon. He begged off the invitation to tea, joking that it was late enough in the day for whiskey. Bones was happy to see his car back in his driveway without a scratch. Eli fell asleep in his clothes before he could have dinner and slept until midnight. Then he was wide awake.

He changed into his jeans, made himself a sandwich, and found Bones still working over a corpse in the mortuary embalming room.

"I was afraid I'd find you here," he said. "I thought you had, you know, people to do this."

The body was a 14-year old African-American boy. There was a bullet wound in his chest the medics hadn't had time to dress before he expired.

"I like to keep my hand in, so to speak," Bones said. "Sad joke. See how gray he looks? We can't even turn white when we're dead. You, you can't do it."

"Turn white or win the case? You think we're going to lose?"

"No, I mean, no way you're turning black. You can't know what it's like. Unless you get stopped in the middle of the night for no reason except being who you are. And you die, you just get whiter."

"What happened to him?"

"Drive-by. Wrong place, wrong time. Now get outta here. I got to chocolate him up for his mama."

~

SINCE THE HEARING wasn't set to resume until that afternoon, Bones suggested a friendly game of one-on-one over at the court on the elementary school playground. Eli thought he was on his game, although neither had scored yet, when he faked right, spun left, and executed a nearly perfect shot from outside the key. But it bounced off the rim, and Bones caught it.

The missed shot fouled Eli's mood. "They wouldn't believe Cyndi if she showed them a video," he fumed.

They decided to call it quits. Just then, Ramon tore by on his skateboard wearing his bright red backpack.

"Hola! Abogado!" he cried out.

"Hey, Ramon!" Eli called after him. "Get your scrawny self back here." Then, to Bones, he asked, "Why would a cop be afraid of a ten-year-old kid?"

Bones shrugged. "They insisted he doesn't know anything. What *could* he know?"

Ramon protested he'd be late for school, but Eli sat him down on a bench and relieved him of the backpack.

"We need to check it out, bro. You know at the school they worry you smuggle in, I don't know what. But they worry. I just want to keep you out of trouble."

"They're not going to like you fooling with it," he said. "But you being my lawyer, I guess it's okay."

His back to Ramon, Eli unzipped the bag and pulled out a coffee can. As Bones looked on, they found the can filled with a huge wad of hundred-dollar bills. Eli quickly sealed the can back up just the way he found it, wiped his prints off with the tail of his T-shirt, and zipped the bag closed.

"Do you know what's in here?" Eli asked him.

"Nope. And I'm not supposed to look until lunch."

"And you're planning to take this into the school?"

"Nope. I got a stop to make first."

"Who gave you the coffee can?"

"Same guy gave me the messages for you."

Eli shot Bones a look. "But the can's not for me?"

"I don't know who it's for. I just leave it this place he said. It's not a bomb, is it?"

"No, Ramon. It's not a bomb. But it is kind of against the law, I'm pretty sure." Eli crouched down to the kid's eye level. "Listen, *mi cliente*. You get to ditch school today. Just don't make it a habit. Here's my card."

"I already got one."

"Well, that's another one for in case. I wrote the address of the courthouse on the back. We need you there at two o'clock. A nice lady, the clerk of the court, will write you a note to take to school tomorrow. But remember, we need your mother there, too."

"And it's not, like, dangerous? I'm not some snitch?"

"All you have to do it point to the guy. He'll be there, but he's not about to hurt you or anyone." Eli handed him the backpack. "I don't want to know where you're supposed to take this. Just make sure it gets there. Don't tell anyone you saw us, then go straight home. If your mother has any questions, she can call me."

"Do I have to make a speech?"

"No," Eli said. "Just point at the guy when I ask, and you're done."

After the boy skated off, Bones said, "I don't like involving the kid in this."

"We didn't get him involved," Eli said. "They did."

Spectators milled outside the hearing room. The bailiff opened the big doors from the inside, and they all filed in.

Eli stood talking with Keiko and checked his watch. Ten minutes to gavel, and Ferrara was always prompt.

"We haven't been able to say much to each other," Eli said. "I mean, of a personal nature."

"Of a personal nature?" She smiled. "I love it when you talk dirty. But to be honest, I'm not sure yet what there is to say.

You have enough to think about getting through all this. After we know what's what, you can buy me a glass of wine and tell me why you think *you* dumped *me*."

How about a bottle, or maybe two?

On the other side of the gleaming marble hallway, Nichols was conferring with Torres.

As if cued by some movie director, the elevator door beside them opened, and out came Ramon in his Sunday best accompanied by his mother, Lupe. Eli had already had polite dealings with her when he'd paid a call to inform her about the baseball incident.

"Thanks for bringing him, Mrs. Rodriguez," he said.

"Are you sure he's not in any trouble? He wouldn't tell me what this is about. He just said you said he had to be here."

"Ramon is the star of the show today. This won't take long, and he goes back to school tomorrow."

He asked Keiko to help them find a seat. As the boy and his mother went with her, Eli cast a look to Torres, who didn't seem fazed by the appearance of Ramon. Nichols had already gone in.

Either the guy is good at poker, or somehow I figured wrong.

Oates emerged from the bathroom, leaning on his cane as he limped. He caught sight of Ramon and did a double-take. Then he went over to Torres and took him aside.

Oates walked away, but not into the hearing room. Eli lingered to see what Torres would do.

Maybe the guy will want to chat?

But Torres went into the men's room, and Eli followed right behind.

Torres stood at the mirror and combed his hair, a pointless thing to do to a brush-cut.

"It was your idea, wasn't it?" Eli asked him. "Use a kid from my neighborhood. Try to warn me off. We drop the case, nobody gets hurt."

"I've got nothing to say to you," he said.

"You had plenty to say when you were sending messages through Ramon."

"Where did you get the idea I'm your friend?"

"I thought you were a guy who knows about honor."

"Honor? I don't want a medal. I got a drawer full of them. What I want is to get home in one piece, every day, one day after the next, until I can retire early, fully vested. Then I'll sell houses or play golf. And try to forget I ever saw you."

And he left.

And in came Oates with his cane. No sooner was he in than he shoved a book of matches between the door and the jamb so it wouldn't open from the outside.

Eli rushed forward to reach for the door handle, but Oates grabbed his wrist, spun him around, and then snapped the cane up to Eli's neck just as Keiko had done to Purvis with the baton.

"You can't scream," he said. "You can't get enough air."

Oates let up on the pressure just enough for Eli to croak out, "What's going on?"

"I should ask you," he said. "You plan to put some beaner kid on the stand? You behave, you don't cry out, I'll let you breathe, and we'll have a conversation. And then maybe you will make it out of here."

"It was Torres. Talking through Ramon. Feeling guilty, trying to warn me."

"Answer the question."

"All Ramon has to do is point out the guy who gave him the messages for me. I'm guessing sending him on other errands was some scheme of yours. But it was Rob at the cemetery, Rob who gave Ramon the notes for me."

"Like we said, those were warnings."

"Torching my Mustang?"

"Student protesters have done worse for less reason."

"I kept asking myself. What would make some tough cops afraid of a little ten-year-old kid? That age, they can only be useful to you guys a few ways. Informers and mules. You get him to carry messages, you find he's reliable. What else can he carry in that backpack of his? Drugs? Cash? Jewelry? 'The kid doesn't know anything,' you said. Oh, yeah? He knows where he goes. You guys are doing business on the side."

Oates let his cane fall to his side. "No one was ever out to kill you or your little lady. But nobody could mind if we scared you shitless. Of course, we're past that now."

"Of course. What about Danny Ellis? Somebody scared the life out of him."

"You got no reason to believe me, but that wasn't us. He hung out with wrong guys. And he wasn't particularly smart. And I could tell you the mule thing is an undercover operation you nearly blew, but you'll never know, and frankly, I don't care what you think. The kid points out Rob, it doesn't prove anything. Ferrara will rule it's irrelevant, and it is."

"You'd take the chance she'll leave it on the record? Make it easy for some investigator down the line? I'm not here to get you for every wrong thing you've ever done," Eli said. "I care about what you did to Hank. Let's say I don't put Ramon on the stand. Let's say we don't talk about messages or coffee or corruption of a minor or anything the jury isn't supposed to think about. What is it you want? I can't change the facts, but if you've got anything you want to say, I'll make sure they hear it."

"All anyone owes a cop is respect. Can you give me that?"

IN THE HEARING ROOM, Oates took a seat in the back near Torres, Nichols, and Hughes. It was a row of black uniforms. Oates studied Eli, who conferred with Bones and Marcia. The jury was in place, and as the last of the visitors came in, a news crew tried to bring in a camera, but the bailiff sent them back out.

Sandoval had not bothered to show up.

Ferrara sat down and immediately gaveled for quiet. "Ladies and gentlemen, we'll have order. There being no further witnesses –"

"Ms. Ferrara," Eli interrupted, "we wish to recall a witness. Officer Norbert Oates."

Sitting beside Eli, Bones was startled and whispered, "Are you crazy?"

"He's dying to do this," Eli said softly. "Poor Ramon is not getting his day in court after all." In fact, Eli had already sent the boy home with a new ten-dollar bill, along with the promised note of excuse from the clerk. "Who says we can't pay witnesses?"

Michelson rose to say, "Your honor, Officer Oates has asserted his Fifth Amendment rights. What possible purpose could this serve?"

"Mr. Michelson," Eli said, "I assure you I care more about Officer Oates' rights than he does. I believe he wants to present his version of the facts."

Ferrara asked, "Is Officer Oates present?"

Oates got up, steadying himself with the cane.

Maybe he needs it after all.

"Yes, ma'am," he said.

Michelson studied the cop's face. When Oates gave him a quick nod, he said, "No objection," and sat back down.

"All right," Ferrara said, and she was just as perplexed. "Recall Officer Norbert Oates."

Oates walked regally forward, his majestic pace aided by the cane. By his bearing, he was the distinguished senior officer come to set the record straight.

"Officer Oates," Ferrara said, "you are still under oath. Although there is no charge against you, through your attorney, you have asserted your Fifth Amendment rights. Do you understand you need not answer any question that might require you to give evidence that would implicate you in a crime? Even if you feel you are innocent?"

"I understand," he said and sat down.

"Mr. Wolff," she said, "you may proceed."

This is going to curl some hair. Pray this guy wants to be right more than he needs to play it safe.

"Officer Oates, when you indulged me recently with a demonstration of the choke hold, for a second there I thought I was going to die. I don't often have occasion to feel that way. But in your work, during an average shift on an average day, how many times would you say you worry that you might die the very next moment?"

"Every. Goddamn. Minute." was the quick reply.

He has their attention.

Approaching Oates, Eli said, "I'm going to pose a hypothetical."

"Be my guest."

"If Hank Ellis was as dangerous as you say – if, for example, you thought he had a weapon – and he was resisting arrest – if you felt that your life was in imminent danger – or if you thought he could kill your partner right then – what's the lawful procedure?"

"Use deadly force."

"You mean, beat him to death?"

"No, sir. You use your weapon, and you shoot to kill."

"And you wouldn't hesitate?"

"You hesitate, you die."

"If you were trying to take Mr. Ellis into custody, you

suddenly feared for your life, and you shot him dead – your actions would be correct in every way?"

"Yes, that's how we're trained."

"And he's just as dead from choking as from shooting, is he not?"

"That he is."

Eli took a deep breath before he continued, "You know, Officer Oates, now that I think about it, I realize I've misjudged you. I can't object to your decision to kill Hank Ellis!"

The reaction from the visitors was loud, and it was angry.

"Order!" Ferrara yelled as she gaveled repeatedly.

Eli lowered his voice, but no so much that the room couldn't hear, and came close to Oates. "You went in there to subdue and arrest him. And partway through the struggle, you must have realized – huge man that he was – no way could you guys take him. You're saying you did what any officer is authorized to do in those circumstances. Killing him was simple self-defense!"

"Damn right it was!"

Evans and the church crowd were fuming. Even the jury seemed distressed.

Michelson shot up, "Objection! Move to strike!"

"We will have order!" Ferrara shouted as she gaveled. "Officer Oates. Your answer is potentially incriminating. I must ask you now, if you did not understand the question, your answer will be stricken from the record, and we will stand in recess until you have the opportunity to seek advice of counsel."

Oates waved it off. "I already fly a desk. What more can they do to me?"

Eli held up his palm toward the visitors as if his gesture would be more effective at calming them.

"Officer, I can't blame you for defending yourself."

More murmurs, just when they'd almost settled down.

Eli went on, "But I do blame you for going in there with the intent to brutally punish an innocent man – for the crime of, I believe they call it, 'contempt of cop?'"

Quickly and quietly, Oates could not keep himself from saying, "That was an error in judgment."

Eli gave it a moment, and the room went quiet.

"I'll say," he said. "Nothing further, your honor. We're done."

Oates' eyes were wet, his face flushed. He heaved a big sigh. Marcia Ellis was crying.

Ferrara couldn't help looking over at Nichols. Her expression said something like, "I tried." Sandoval had been absent the whole time and was not to be seen again anywhere near those proceedings.

Ferrara took a breath and then addressed the jury: "The law requires that you must find whether the decedent's death was by – one, natural causes – two, suicide – three, accident – or four, at the hands of another person other than by accident. You may now commence your deliberations. This hearing will adjourn until you have reached your determination."

On his way out of the hearing room, Eli was accosted by a TV news reporter, the first he'd seen since the early days of the case. As the crew waved a camera and mic in Eli's face, the guy asked, "Any comment, sir? I guess that's it for today. We figure it's going to be a while."

"No comment," Eli said. "Except I've got a piece of a dollar that says you're wrong."

ELI INSISTED it would soon be over, so he, Bones, and Keiko lingered in the hallway with Marcia.

"You had me going there," Marcia said. "For a minute I didn't know whose side you were on."

"My man Eli grew himself a humongous set of black balls," Bones said. "And he didn't scratch my rims on the curb. He's all right."

The newsman called out, "Jury's back!"

"What was that?" Bones checked his watch. "Fourteen minutes?"

"Why does nobody take my bets?" Eli quipped.

Bones asked him, "Does that mean you think we won?"

"It means I think they'd didn't have to think about it very much. Which either means they had their minds made up from the beginning – bad – or we scored there at the last – good – or the whole thing is wired – very, very bad. In that case, I might just apply for a job as an apprentice mortician."

"You could come to work at the clinic," Keiko said, and he wasn't sure it was a joke.

JONAS, the jury foreman, read from a file card, which must have had the official language in a fill-in-the-blanks-type form: "We the jurors summoned before this inquest find that one Henry Ellis, aged twenty-nine, came to his death on September fourth at his residence and that this death was caused by strangulation."

The visitors could not restrain their joy, and Ferrara had to gavel them down before the foreman could continue.

"And from the testimony introduced, we find this death to have been at the hands of another person, other than by accident."

It was difficult to hear Ferrara pronounce the conclusion of the proceedings.

At the counsel's table, Eli embraced the sobbing Marcia.

Evans rushed over, also in tears, and announced, "Never again! You da man!"

"It's a start," Eli said.

Bones and Keiko joined them, and he asked Eli, "Can I kiss Keiko?"

"Why are you asking me? I've got no claim on her." He meant it as a joke.

"Yes, he does," she said. "But kiss me anyway."

24

The day after the coroner's office announced its findings, the case got a paragraph on page twelve of the mainstream paper. A reporter from a paper in the community left a phone message he wanted a quote, but Eli hadn't yet returned the call. He'd promised to buy Keiko a lavish lunch, but first he thought he should take care of old business and drop by the halfway house.

Vince greeted him with, "I take it all back. You won bigtime."

"There's talk of a settlement, which is best for the widow and her kids. And the politicians know that's the way to keep things quiet and move on."

"It won't make you Mister Popular downtown," Vince said. "You going back to chasing ambulances?"

"Victims' rights might be an area. We'll have to see." Then he said, "I wish I had better news for Gabe."

Oddly, Vince smiled. "I'll get him and we'll all go for a beer."

THE UGLY ROSE was a blue-collar bar within walking distance of the house. They could hardly discriminate against Latinos, but the only beers they had on tap were Pabst Blue Ribbon and Hamm's. Gabe asked for a bottle of Corona and got a look colder than the beer turned out to be.

Eli asked him, "Do you even get to drink? I mean, aren't we breaking some law?"

"Not when the parole officer is buying," Vince said. "If I want to put it on my expense report, I'll have to say it was sandwiches. Which is not a bad idea either. They got sausage with peppers and onions. Philly cheese-steak. On rolls from some bakery. The pizza is a disappointment."

There was a moment of hallowed silence as they gulped their beers. Then Eli said to Gabe, "I'm sorry I don't have anything for you."

"I figure you tried," Gabe said. He didn't look particularly upset.

"There were five kids named Marco Gutierrez in the system, going back some years. None of with the middle name Julio and none with the birthdate you gave me. I can't explain it."

"You don't have to," Gabe said as he shot a look to Vince. "I guess you can't fix everybody."

Eli asked Vince, "Tell me. Why couldn't you dive into this for him? I didn't mind, but I bet you have better access than I do."

"Did you give it a lot of thought? Feel like you were chasing your tail?"

"Hell, yes. My mind was swimming in all this garbage from the case, and then before I closed my eyes each night, I'm obsessing over baby Marco."

"So, it gave you something to think about besides the case?" Vince asked.

"You know, it was amazing," Eli said. "I couldn't turn my mind off. When I finally got to sleep, I'd be out for the duration. You'd think it would add to the stress, but it was just the opposite."

Vince smiled. So did Gabe.

"Gabe, I'm truly sorry I came up empty," Eli said. "I just don't know where to go with this. As far as the record is concerned, little Marco never existed."

Gabe's smile became a laugh, then Vince joined in.

"That's because he didn't," Gabe said.

Eli took a sink-in moment before he said, "You guys punked me?"

Vince yelled out, "Hey, Boss!"

From a booth in the back where he'd been sitting facing the wall, a familiar black man stood up and sauntered over to them.

"These guys are just accomplices. You have been punked once more by Luther Jackson Junior."

"You sick, sorry, son of a –"

Bones sat down and signaled to Darla, the middle-aged white barmaid, for another round.

"But the story about Pilar. That was true?"

"Not at all," Gabe said. "Award-winning fiction, looks like."

"Why?" Eli asked.

"Sometimes, my friend," Bones said, "all there is between the lines is white space. You deserve your win, but don't think you can ever figure it all out. Best chase your new wisdom with a shot of humility."

Vince said, "Gabe's going to be back out on the street soon, and you can count him as one of your homies now."

And they drank.

25

Dear Lucille,

Well, I've changed my mind. I know that's something you don't expect men to do all that much. I didn't tell you about it, but my partner and I were involved in an incident. It happens all the time – you have to deal with a violent situation, and then they second-guess you forever afterward. I don't know anyone who has been on the force any length of time who hasn't been put on desk duty a few times while they make sure it was a righteous thing.

Even when they tell you you're okay and you can go back to the beat, you won't be sure yourself. You did what was necessary, you thought, but you play it in your mind over and over. You have upsetting dreams. You wake in the middle of the night.

In this case, they put me on desk duty all through this trial. They called it an inquest, but it's still a court proceeding with all the legal nonsense. I was bored out of my skull doing the desk job, and all the while the pain in my leg is getting worse. I suppose with all the stress that piece of shrapnel is working its way around, and then there's inflammation and a world of hurt. Painkillers didn't do much, and it had me going back to walking with a cane.

When I was on patrol, I'd think eight or ten or even twelve hours would be over before it started. Sitting on that desk, I'm working through a stack of paper, and it's like it takes forever. I work through one report, I look up at the clock, and not ten minutes have gone by. I don't know how people do it. I really don't.

They offered me early retirement, and I decided to take it. I did the math, and they'll actually be paying me more *not* to work. The ending of the case wasn't all that clear-cut, I guess, and they'd just as soon I was out of the picture.

Let me know when might be a good time to pay a visit. Brad and I can take some time. Maybe he's ready to talk to me, and me to him. Then he should finish out the year. We don't want to be pulling him out. So, come summer, if he wants to come back here, I'll find us a house to rent, and we'll take it from there.

I'm grateful. You know it.

Your loving brother,

Bert

26

E li bought a new Ford Thunderbird two-door Heritage Coupe. He thought it looked sporty but more conservative than his toasted sportscar. Under the hood was a Mustang 302 cubic-inch V8 engine that put out 157 horsepower. He and Keiko were once again driving in the direction of a resort town, not quite so late at night. On a stretch of deserted road, he was tempted to open up the throttle to find out whether this new bucket of bolts had as much to give as his old one.

"A man gets some money, and the first thing he thinks about is buying a new car," Keiko teased.

"Sure. My second thought was I'd invest in the clinic. Child abuse is an area of the law that needs some work. It would be a good way to work together."

"Is that your idea of a proposal? Some kind of joint business venture?"

"It is, if you like the idea."

Flashing lights appeared behind them.

"Uh-oh," Eli said.

"How fast were you going?"

As he pulled over, he said, "Seriously, I have no idea. You kind of had me distracted."

She said, "Be careful. And respectful."

"Hey," he said. "It's a done deal. They can't touch us now."

A police officer strode up to the driver's window and bent down.

It was Rob Torres.

"Keiko, it's Rob!" Eli lowered the window.

"License and registration" was all he said.

Eli pulled his license from his wallet, and Keiko handed over the registration from the glove compartment. He handed them through the window to Rob.

"Stay where you are," Torres said.

In his side mirror, Eli could see Rob walk back to a black limousine as it pulled up behind the squad car. The officer stood talking for several minutes at the rear passenger door of the limo.

"Hell of a coincidence," Eli said. "Since when do these guys make highway stops? And out here?"

Keiko was shaken. "What's *he* doing on patrol? If he's back in uniform, something's wrong. He should still be on desk duty. Who's he talking to?"

Torres walked back to the Thunderbird, his boots crunching on the gravel of the shoulder.

Leaning back down at the window, Torres said to Eli, "Get out of the car. Slowly. You stand at the back. And, Miss, you stand at the front."

They hesitated, but then they did as they were told.

Eli walked with Torres to the back of the vehicle and noticed he'd forgotten to turn off the headlights. The taillights bathed the scene in an eerie, red glow. As they reached the space between the cars, Torres looked straight at Eli and let the license and registration fall from his hand to the ground.

Unclipping the baton from his waist, Torres said, "Pick up your documents, sir."

"Look, Rob –"

Torres didn't answer, didn't move. Eli bent slowly down but tried to keep looking up.

The baton swung in a powerful arc, just missing Eli's head and connecting *CRACK!* as it shattered the left rear taillight into a shower of glittering fragments.

Eli had fallen on his hands, the gravel digging into his palms as he still clutched the papers.

Torres used the club to point to the broken taillight.

"Best watch your back, sir," he said.

With a curt nod, Torres turned and walked slowly back to his squad car. The idling engine of the limo revved.

Shakily, Eli began to stand. The squad car pulled out and passed him, speeding down the road.

Keiko came back to see he was safe, her face wet with tears. When he was standing, she took him in her arms gently.

Then the limo glided past them slowly. The shadowy figure of the passenger in the back seat was just barely visible behind the smoked glass.

As the limo pulled away, Eli read the license plate: *LAW 1*.

And he remembered what Bones had told him:

You can't know what it's like... unless you get stopped... in the middle of the night... for no reason... except being who you are.

EPILOGUE

You'd think that Eli's sensational result in the case would have changed history. It did not.

The Hank Ellis case was settled out of court. Financial compensation of more than a million dollars was awarded to the man's widow and family. It was among the first settlements with any big city in the nation for which compensation was paid to a victim for wrongful death by police. However, because there was never a criminal trial, the murder and its proof remain presumptive. And because the settlement was reached before the finding of the inquest could be entered in to the city's official records, the coroner's opinion that the decedent had died from heart failure from the stress of being taken into custody was never altered.

The two officers were placed on probationary desk duty for a time. No charges were ever brought against either of them.

After the case was no longer in the news, the medical examiner's office discontinued its usual practice of conducting inquests, including cases that might involve police misconduct. Officer-involved killings were investigated by an internal affairs group inside the department, but facts were rarely reviewed or debated in public.

Flash forward a few more decades, to recent times. There has been a series of high-profile police shootings in major cities all over the country, along with subsequent riots and demonstrations. Some sociologists, politicians, medical examiners, and law-enforcement officials have recommended resumption of the inquest process. The purpose would not be to replace police internal investigations or criminal proceedings – but to provide a prompt, transparent examination and a way for the decedent's family and the community to review and discuss the facts and circumstances. The hope is that an inquest could help prevent misinformation and rumor from stirring up hatred and violence.

Meanwhile, every so often the death of an inmate will be explained by a coroner's report that seems little more than a cut-and-paste version of Sandoval's finding in Ellis.

That is, many people of color seem prone to dying of heart failure when prison guards or police are attempting to bring them under control.

ABOUT THE AUTHOR

 Gerald Everett Jones is a freelance writer who lives in Santa Monica, California. He is a board member of the Writers & Publishers Network and host of the GetPublished! Radio podcast. He holds a Bachelor of Arts with Honors from the College of Letters, Wesleyan University, where he studied under novelists Peter Boynton *(Stone Island)*, F.D. Reeve *(The Red Machines)*, and Jerzy Kosinski *(The Painted Bird, Being There)*.

Find out more at **geraldeverettjones.com.** Read his interviews and blog posts at Thinking About Thinking on Substack @geraldeverettjones.

Photo by Gabriella Muttone Photography, Hollywood

ALSO BY GERALD EVERETT JONES

Fiction

Jonathan's Journal: A novel

Harry Harambee's Kenyan Sundowner: A Novel – Multiple awards in Literary Fiction

Preacher Finds a Corpse (Evan Wycliff #1) – Multiple awards in Mystery

Preacher Fakes a Miracle (Evan Wycliff #2) – NYC Big Book Silver 2020

Preacher Raises the Dead (Evan Wycliff #3) – Multiple awards in Mystery

Preacher Stalls the Second Coming (Evan Wycliff #4)

Mick & Moira & Brad: A Romantic Comedy - Multiple awards in Romantic Comedy

Clifford's Spiral: A Novel – IPA Silver in Literary Fiction 2020

Mr. Ballpoint – Page Turner Award in Fiction Finalist 2022 *Christmas*

Karma – WGA Diversity Award (Screenplay) 2016 *Choke Hold: An Eli*

Wolff Thriller
Bonfire of the Vanderbilts: A Novel / *Bonfire of the Vanderbilts: Scholar's Edition*

My Inflatable Friend (Misadventures of Rollo Hemphill #1) *Rubber*

Babes (Misadventures of Rollo Hemphill #2)

Farnsworth's Revenge (Misadventures of Rollo Hemphill #3)

Stories and Essay *Boychik Lit*

Nonfiction

How to Lie with Charts - Eric Hoffer Award Finalist in Business 2020

The Death of Hypatia and the End of Fate

The Light in His Soul: Lessons from My Brother's Schizophrenia (with Rebecca Schaper)

Searching for Jonah: Clues in Hebrew and Assyrian History by Don E. Jones (Afterword)

RECENT AWARD-WINNING RELEASES

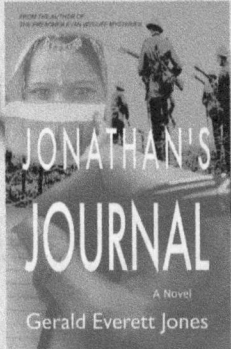